ELIZABETH McGINTY

◆

HER FORGOTTEN LOVE

Complete and Unabridged

LINFORD
Leicester

First published in Great Britain in 2019

First Linford Edition
published 2020

A catalogue record for this book is available
from the British Library.

ISBN 978–1–4448–4523–5

Published by
Ulverscroft Limited
Anstey, Leicestershire

Set by Words & Graphics Ltd.
Anstey, Leicestershire
Printed and bound in Great Britain by
T. J. International Ltd., Padstow, Cornwall

This book is printed on acid-free paper

Unexpected Crisis

Elisa thanked her lucky stars as she spotted a parking space right outside her block of flats, and negotiated her car into the place. Switching off the engine, she noticed that her flat was in darkness.

She guessed Michael, her partner, had gone to bed and not thought to leave a light on for her return.

Unlocking the front door she entered the hall area, thankful to be home at last.

Through the glow thrown from the outside security light, she noticed the mail sitting on the hall table but was too tired to open it.

Tiptoeing through the semi-darkness she made it to the living-room. Sinking into her comfy sofa she flicked on the lamp on the side table, and kicked off her shoes.

It had been a very long working day. She enjoyed her job as assistant general manager for a chain of quality hotels but today she had started with the breakfast shift, and continued until the last dinner guests had been served.

One benefit of working in a hotel was eating her meals in her workplace, so she didn't need to cook for herself.

With great reluctance, Elisa raised her tired body from the sofa, limped to the other side of the room, and closed the blinds in her cosy one-bedroomed flat.

Moving to the bathroom she ran herself a bath. As she collected fresh towels, she peeped into the bedroom. She smiled at the sight of Michael sound asleep in their bed. He looked so handsome. His normally tidy hair was curled against his pillow and his chin had just enough stubble for her to want to brush her cheek against it.

The sheet had slipped exposing his bare muscular chest and arms, and for a moment she was almost tempted to abandon all thoughts of her bath and just creep in beside him.

Forcing herself into the hot soapy water of the bath she allowed her body to relax, and felt the exhaustion melt away. She thought of the long hours she and Michael worked to build their future.

They had moved in together six months ago. Michael worked as a mechanic at a nearby garage, and Elisa's shifts often meant they had little time together. They tried to make sure the time they did share was enjoyable.

As she stood up from the bath she felt more relaxed. She wrapped her body in a warm thick towel, and ruffled her hair as she moved silently to the bedroom.

★　★　★

Elisa awoke to sunlight peeping through the window blind. Reaching for Michael, she discovered his side of the bed lay empty.

She glanced at the bedside clock and

realised he had long ago left for work, leaving her asleep.

Stretching her arms above her head, she smiled, pleased that she didn't need to go to work until lunchtime. Not wishing to waste the morning, Elisa decided to get the household tasks done before heading to the gym prior to her shift starting.

Housework in the flat didn't take long as she kept it neat and tidy. Michael also contributed to his share of the tasks so she whizzed through it in no time.

As she put the washing in the tumble drier, she was surprised to find fluff in the filter as she was meticulous about cleaning it. Shrugging it off, she decided she warranted a break, and treated herself to a coffee.

As she was enjoying the luxury of time to herself, she remembered the mail from the previous night.

It still lay where she had left it. She shook her head that Michael left everything for her to open. Amongst the junk mail, she found a letter post-marked Italy and her heart skipped a beat as she recognised the scratchy handwriting of her beloved nonno, her Italian grandfather Stephano.

She was at once transported to her grandfather's home in Italy where she lived before moving to England to study. As she read his letter her spirits lifted as he told her stories of the staff at his hotel.

She was pleased he wrote again about his friend Cesare, but she was confused that he wrote about him as though Elisa had met him. It was clear they seemed to enjoy each other's company. She smiled at how much love he was sending her, and was pleased she would soon be visiting him.

Elisa was happy with her life in England, but she often yearned to be back in Italy in her grandfather's hotel, the Hotel Villa Perlino, where she had been brought up by her grandfather and grandmother. She missed the familiarity that came with it.

She felt tears prick her eyes then she reminded herself it was only ten days to go before she would see Stephano and gauge exactly how he was.

Searching the letter for further clues to his well-being, she wondered how she could persuade him to slow down a little, and she knew she would have a fight on her hands trying.

The ringing of her mobile phone brought her out of her daydream with a start.

'Hi,' she said, smiling into the phone as she recognised Michael's number.

'Elisa,' Michael said, 'don't panic, I'm at Accident and Emergency. A bit of equipment slipped, and it fell on to my arm. It might need to be stitched.'

'I'll be right there,' Elisa said as she hurried to get her bag and car keys.

'No, there's no need,' Michael said and then let out a small groan.

'I'm on my way.'

'Thanks, babe.'

* * *

6

'Are you OK?' Elise asked Michael for about the 100th time that night.

'Yeah, just a bit sore now the anaesthetic's wearing off.' Michael winced as he answered. 'I'm sorry — you shouldn't have cancelled your shift.'

'Of course I needed to cancel my shift, silly.' She stroked his hair. 'Who else was going to pander to your every need when you're feeling so sore?' She lightly brushed her lips against his and then quickly moved out of his reach, before he tried to move his injured arm to catch her.

'Tease,' he shouted after her.

'I'm just a good nurse.' She laughed back. 'I need to go to work first thing tomorrow to make up for today. I'll try not to disturb you.'

* * *

'So how is Michael?' Fiona, Elise's colleague and best friend since university, asked when they arrived to begin their morning shift at the hotel.

'He's bearing up. I've left him with loads of drinks, snacks and painkillers with the TV remote control to hand so I'm sure he'll survive until I get home.' Elise smiled back. 'Thanks for covering my shift last night, I'll make it up to you.'

'You know you don't need to do that. You're for ever helping me out with shifts when I have childcare issues,' Fiona said.

'Well I can't disappoint my gorgeous god-daughter.' Elise laughed.

'You know, Elisa, the hotel isn't too busy today and we have enough staff to cover. Why don't you head back home after the breakfast rush? Ava is having a fun-with-Daddy day so I'm free to cover any emergencies that might happen.'

'Are you sure, Fiona? I bet Ava is running rings around her daddy. It would be helpful if I can at least have a day at home whilst Michael's arm is still out of action.'

'Go before I change my mind.' Fiona

shooed her friend away.

Elisa gave her friend a quick hug of thanks, and went to collect her things before heading home.

Shocking Discovery

Elisa pulled up outside the flat. The road was busy with cars so she parked further up the street than she would have liked. Carrying a bundle of car magazines and chocolate bars she almost ran upstairs towards their first-floor home.

As Elisa skipped up the stairs she imagined Michael's suggestions on how they could fill the rest of the day. Unlocking the front door, she resisted shouting a greeting in case he was sleeping.

Moving in silence into the dark and quiet bedroom, her smile froze on her face at the sight in front of her. Michael was sound asleep, his rugged face unshaven against the pillow, but curled up beside him under the bedclothes and watching Elisa with interest and a challenging stare, was a female Elisa

10

had never seen before.

As an uncontrolled gasp left Elisa's throat, she clasped her hands over her mouth, shocked and unable to make sense of the scene in her own bedroom.

Michael stirred and turned towards his female companion, throwing a muscular arm around her unclothed body.

'Oh, Lauren,' he whispered. As he turned his head to snuggle into the female, he caught sight of Elisa standing at the foot of the bed. Colour drained from his face, and he struggled to sit up, realisation dawning on his flustered face.

Gathering all the civility she could, Elisa looked directly at the woman.

'I'll wait in the car. Please put your clothes on and leave my home.' She turned to Michael. 'I'll be back in ten minutes. I suggest you get dressed too.'

Waiting in the car, her body shaking, a sudden thought came to Elisa as she recollected putting washing in the tumble drier the previous day. She had noticed the filter contained bits of pink fluff.

Elisa always made sure the filter was kept clean, just as she had been taught during the many health and safety training courses she attended at the hotel.

Now a chill moved up her spine as she realised the fluff was from the bed sheets. This affair between Michael and this woman had been going on right under her nose, and Michael had been devious enough to try to cover his tracks. How could she have been such a fool?

She thought she and Michael were happy. They had made a commitment to buy their first home together. Hot tears rolled down her cheeks and as she brushed them away, she came to a decision.

Reaching for her mobile phone, Elisa dialled the airline, and arranged a flight to Italy. She was going home to her grandfather, and Hotel Villa Perlino. As she spoke to the airline operator, Elisa saw a taxi pull up and the woman Michael had called Lauren so passionately, took her time descending the entrance stairs and strutted towards it.

It looked to Elisa like a deliberate act of provocation, and that was confirmed as Lauren turned towards Elisa's car and shot a look of defiance towards her before stepping into the cab.

Given the distance Elisa was parked from the flat entrance, she realised Lauren knew which car to look for and she felt unsettled.

Elisa gripped the steering wheel to regain her composure, before she headed back to her flat to confront Michael. She sighed as, with shaking hands, she once more slipped the key into the lock, unable to grasp all that had occurred in the last ten minutes.

Michael met her in the hall.

'Elisa, I'm sorry. I wasn't expecting you home.' He stood in front of her unable to meet her gaze.

'Is that the best you can do, Michael? Is this somehow my fault I've just caught you in bed with that woman?' Elisa willed herself to remain in control. Moving towards the bedroom she began throwing clothes into a case.

'What are you doing? Wait, Elisa, let's talk. There's no need to make rash decisions.' Michael followed her around the room. 'Why are you taking your passport?'

'Because, Michael, I am leaving. I'm worth more than . . . ' She threw her arms towards the unmade bed. 'That.'

Michael sat down on the bed, his head slumped in his hands.

'I'm sorry, Elisa. I never meant to hurt you. I'm not sure how this has all happened.'

'Well, it has, Michael. I trusted you, and now . . . well, I don't think I could ever trust you again.' Elisa gathered up her case, collected her mail and without a backward glance she left the flat.

Once in her car she drew in deep breaths to force herself to stop shaking, then starting the engine she headed back to the hotel.

* * *

Fiona was surprised to see Elisa back at the hotel so soon, but one glance at her face showed something was wrong.

Elisa was thankful the staff room was empty and the hotel quiet as she poured out to her friend all that had happened.

'I can't believe he could do that to me, Fiona. I've spoken to head office and they've agreed I can bring my annual leave forward to let me go visit my grandfather. I really need to see him right now, Fiona. I can't explain it.'

'Of course. You do whatever you feel you need to do right now. We'll manage here, and Joe and I can collect anything you need from the flat,' Fiona said.

'Thank you. Please give Ava a big hug from me, and tell her I'll see her soon,' Elisa said as a tear rolled down her cheek. 'I'll miss her so much.'

'It won't be for long,' Fiona said, 'and my parents will spoil her in your absence.'

'Of course you're right, Fiona. I just need time to think and speak with my grandfather — he always knows how to fix things.' Elisa gave her friend a smile as she got up to leave. 'I'll be back soon.'

Tragic Reunion

In the busy airport, Elisa re-read the recent letter from Stephano. She knew he would be pleased to see her earlier than arranged. Stephano loomed large in her life, stepping in to provide her with a home following the tragic loss of her mother and father.

He was old now, too old to be running a hotel, when he should have been enjoying his retirement. Trying to persuade Stephano to retire was futile. He lived for his hotel.

Elisa looked forward to meeting his friend Cesare, too. Maybe between them they could persuade Stephano to take things easier.

Just as she was daydreaming about Italy she heard her mobile ring. She ignored it, expecting it to be Michael again.

Since she had walked out, Michael

had phoned hourly, pleading with her to meet with him.

The memories of the moment she caught him cheating on her were too raw in her mind to even contemplate seeing him, and so she ignored his calls and voicemail messages.

Boarding her flight, Elisa vowed to put all thoughts of Michael behind her, and concentrate on her grandfather. With a flourish, she switched her phone off.

Her spirits lifted as she realised that in the space of a short time her priorities were changing. Michael was no longer at the forefront of her mind. Instead she would look forward to seeing Stephano and, even if it was only for a short stay, she was going home.

★   ★   ★

Michael redialled Elisa's number on his mobile phone and held it to his ear. Hearing the voicemail message again he disconnected and threw the phone on to the sofa.

He was confused and angry that he had made such a mess of things. He loved Elisa, but had fallen for the charms, if that was the word, of Lauren when she appeared at the garage a few weeks earlier. She didn't disguise her attraction to him and like a fool he felt flattered.

The buzz of the door intercom made him jump.

'Elisa?' he said as he ran to answer.

'Hi, Michael,' Lauren's husky voice whispered through the speaker. Michael pressed the button and let her in.

★   ★   ★

The flight was quick and uneventful. As the plane landed at Verona airport Elisa felt a weight lift from her shoulders, and her body relaxed.

Stepping off the plane she enjoyed the warmth of the sun on her skin. She made her way through the familiar route to passport control, and on to car rental to collect her prearranged car.

As always, there was a queue of people waiting to complete the necessary paperwork. She took a seat, smiling at the chatter of Italian voices around her. Unexpectedly, she heard her name being called, and turned to be confronted by an unknown man.

'Elisa . . . ' The man came towards her.

'Yes,' Elisa answered, wondering who this person was and how he knew her name.

'You don't remember me, do you, Elisa?' he continued.

Elisa stared at the man. He was over six feet tall, slim build, casually dressed in white open-necked shirt and denims. She guessed he was probably of similar age to herself, maybe early thirties. He had a head of dark curly hair but she couldn't place him.

'No, I'm sorry,' she said, thinking she would most definitely have remembered this attractive man.

'Forgive me, I shouldn't make you play guessing games. I'm Cesare, Cesare Favero. We were at school together before you left to study in England.'

'Cesare — but you were . . . ' Elisa began to say.

'Yes, I know, I was a goofy little runt.' He gave a lopsided grin. 'I just grew taller.'

'No, no, you weren't — and yes, you have.' Elisa tried to hide her confusion, and blushed as she realised she was staring at this handsome man, and was quite thrown that his smile had made her stomach flutter a little.

'How lovely to see you, Cesare,' Elise replied, sorry she wasn't really in the mood for a reunion however good-looking this man was.

'It's Detective Inspector Cesare Favero. Here is my identification.' He looked sheepish at using his formal title.

'Congratulations, Detective Inspector.' Elisa wondered why he needed to prove his identity to her.

As she wondered, she became aware of his arm on her elbow as he led her towards a quiet area. She felt her heart quicken as she sensed something wasn't right.

'Elisa,' he began, 'I've been trying to phone you since yesterday, but you never answered. I knew you were due to fly in today and pulled a few strings to get details.'

She felt rebuked at his tone and regretted not checking her voicemails.

'But why are you looking for me?' Her voice was tight.

'Your nonno is in hospital, he is very ill. It's his heart, I'm afraid.' Cesare laid a gentle hand on her arm.

Elisa shook it off.

'Thank you, I'll go there as soon as they've processed my hire car.' She turned towards the desk, feeling sick inside. Nonno was ill, and she needed to be at his side.

Cesare reached down, and with ease lifted her luggage.

'There's not time. I have the car out

front, follow me.'

Elisa did as he instructed, struggling to keep up with his long strides. As they hurried along, Elisa realised this was the friend her grandfather had written about, her old school friend, but they hadn't seen each other for years, not since they were children.

Forcing his way through the crowded terminal, Cesare led her to a waiting police car. Once inside the car, he switched on the siren and flashing light, negotiating the car through the busy airport traffic and on to the motorway at breakneck speed.

'Now you're frightening me, Cesare,' Elisa said.

'I'm sorry, really I am, but I don't want to waste time,' he replied, staring straight ahead as he concentrated on the busy motorway traffic.

The journey continued in silence. Elisa, terrified by the speed Cesare was driving, realised the urgency of the situation.

Her grandfather needed her, and she

hadn't answered her phone or checked her messages. She was angry she had let him down. Well she would make it up to him now, she thought, now she was home to nurse him back to health.

Cesare mastered his way through the traffic and pulled up at the hospital a short time after leaving the airport.

Reaching down, he assisted Elisa from the car and this time she offered no resistance as he hurried her along the hospital corridors.

They entered the cardiac care ward, which was an oasis of calm in contrast to the chaos of the traffic. A nurse showed them into Stephano's room, and motioned to Elisa to sit in the chair close to the bed.

The nurse spoke in a quiet voice to Stephano, advising him his granddaughter had arrived. Stephano lay pale against the white sheets.

Reaching for his hand, Elisa immediately noticed how fragile he was. This man who had been a giant throughout her life, had shrunk into a smaller version of himself.

As she held his hand his eyes flickered open, and recognition of her made them light up just a little and he smiled.

'I'm here, Nonno, I'm here. You just rest, concentrate on getting well,' Elisa said, thankful for the circumstances leading to her arriving in Italy sooner than expected.

'I love you, Elisa,' he whispered.

'I love you, too, Nonno.' She kissed his hand, the hand that had held her and led her for so many years, now frail and weak as he lay in the hospital bed.

As Elisa sat by him, whispering happy memories merged with prayers, she felt him leave her. Tears fell from her eyes as she cupped his face, and for the last time kissed him goodbye.

'Goodnight, Nonno, take my love with you, until we meet again.' Her heart was heavy, but she was grateful that he was now at peace, and with Nonna, her much-loved grandmother.

Some time passed before Elisa

realised she wasn't alone. Raising her tear-stained face, she found Cesare standing quietly waiting, his eyes glistening with tears.

'I'm so sorry, Elisa,' he said.

'Thank you, Cesare, and thank you for getting me here in time. I didn't know he was so ill.' Elisa began to speak, but her voice wavered. Cesare moved towards her and she fell sobbing into his arms.

Alone in the World

Sighing, Elisa closed and locked the front door of the Hotel Villa Perlino after saying goodbye to the last mourner. She felt drained and exhausted.

Moving to the great wooden reception desk, she ran her fingers along the polished surface as she had done so often in happier times.

She placed her cheek against the cool wood as her eyes rested on the photograph of Stephano, framed and in pride of place on the desk. His warm eyes smiled at her. Picking up the photograph of her beloved grandfather, she held it close to her and cried.

All alone in the world, now that the last person on earth she could call family had gone, Elisa could not contemplate what the future held for her.

The ringing of her mobile echoed through the empty hotel, emphasising her loneliness. Looking at the number she could see it was Fiona, her friend and work colleague. She was tempted to let it go to voicemail, torn between the need for peace and desperation for the sound of a friendly voice.

'Hi, Fiona,' Elisa answered, trying to sound more upbeat than she felt.

'Hi, honey, how are you bearing up? How did it all go?' Fiona's familiar voice questioned her.

'Fine, fine. It all went fine.' Elisa wiped tears from her eyes and face as she spoke.

'I'm sorry I couldn't be there to support you,' Fiona continued. 'My parents were working and I just couldn't get anyone to take care of Ava at short notice. As her godmother, I'm afraid you're my go-to babysitter.'

'I know, Fiona, that's OK. Tell my number one girl I'm sorry I had to rush off. I don't know when I'll be back, there's so much to sort out here.' Elisa stopped short of saying she was in no rush to return.

As if reading her mind Fiona spoke again.

'Michael called me. He sends his condolences. He says you won't return his calls.'

'He can't be surprised, surely! I need time away from him to process what happened.'

'Maybe . . . or perhaps you've already closed that door. Don't forget I've known you a long time, Elisa. I know those Scorpio qualities you have — you're loyal to the extreme but you don't forgive disloyalty easily,' Fiona answered. 'Anyway, I'm sorry I couldn't be there for the funeral but I've put in for some annual leave I'm due and I'm hoping Ava and I could visit to give you some support if that would be OK?'

'Oh, that would be wonderful. I'm sure I have room to put you up.' Elisa tried a weak joke.

'That's more like it. I'll be in touch when I know the arrangements. Bye, honey, see you soon.'

Fiona's words made Elisa think. Had

she really closed the door on her relationship with Michael?

★   ★   ★

As darkness began to fall, the emptiness of the hotel began to close in on her. The usual hustle and bustle of guests and staff had been replaced by a silence she had never before known.

This hotel situated in the little town of Asolto on the edge of Lake Garda in the north of Italy had been in her family for decades. Her grandparents started the business in the 50s out of necessity.

When they married, they lived in a little stone farmhouse which was rented from the farmer, and began to take in bed and breakfast guests to supplement their income from the olive picking.

Eventually, as the tourist industry started to take off, coupled with her grandmother's good cooking, the service and accommodation they offered was making more money than the farming.

Her grandfather was an astute businessman and when an old 10-bedroom house became available in the town, he took a risk, borrowed from the bank and plunged all the family's savings into it.

Elisa remembered how her grandparents Rosa and Stephano often told her stories about the old days and the struggles they endured to keep making payments to the bank and the extra jobs her grandfather worked as he added to the hotel bit by bit.

Meanwhile, all Rosa's time was taken up attending to their guests and, of course, their three children including Elisa's father, Alessandro.

Thinking of her father brought back memories of her parents, her father Alessandro and her mother Grace and the devastating memory of the day she lost them.

Their car skidded off the road as they returned from skiing in the Dolomites.

It fell to her grandparents to raise her, a difficult and angry ten-year-old, as well as deal with their own heartbreak.

It was testament to their strength as a couple that they survived to rebuild a family life with Elisa at the centre of it, and they were her world.

Her memories of her parents faded and with connection with her mother's family in England lost to her, Stephano and Rosa became the only family she knew or needed.

The emptiness left by the loss of their child was filled by the lifelong friendships her grandparents enjoyed with the other villagers and hotel staff as had been apparent in the packed church today.

Elisa tried hard to remember her mother and father but she could only grasp at snippets of conversations and faded scenarios that played around the corners of her mind.

One thing she did remember was the love that enveloped her from her mother and father and the loss she felt when it was snatched so cruelly from her. Now she was back in that situation again, lost and alone.

She reached for another tissue and became aware of a gentle tapping at the front doors. She stopped, unsure if she had heard correctly. No, there it was again.

The hotel was empty as at Elisa's insistence all staff had gone home to their respective families, as they too were devastated on the loss of their much-loved employer. There were no guests as all bookings had been cancelled for a few days and alternative arrangements made in nearby hotels.

For a brief moment she was afraid and all too aware of her isolation. She hesitated, unsure of what she should do. Lifting her mobile phone, she moved towards the hotel entrance.

Her Welfare at Heart

Making her way to the large double glass front doors Elisa could see the tall figure of a man but could not make out the detail. She held her fingers over the keypad of her phone, ready to call for assistance.

The stranger seemed to be holding something in front of him. She could just make out that he was saying, 'It's OK.' Aware of her vulnerability she looked around and lifted a sturdy umbrella from the nearby stand to add to her defences. Cautiously she unlocked a side window and leaned out.

'I'm sorry,' she began to say, 'the hotel is closed, family bereavement,' just as the tall figure of Cesare stepped forward.

Elisa moved to the door and let him in.

'Is there anything wrong?' Elisa's

petite figure was suddenly on alert and she frowned in confusion. 'Why are you here?'

Immediately, Cesare reached out to reassure her and his hand brushed her shoulder, causing them both to pull back.

'I'm sorry, I didn't mean to cause concern. In fact, I'm trying to do the opposite but obviously not very well,' he said. 'I was at your grandfather's service today and it occurred to me to drive by the hotel tonight just to check all was well.'

'That was very kind of you. I'm pleased you're here I didn't get a chance to thank you for all your kindness. Thank you also for being a good friend to him. He spoke of you in his last letter.' Elisa turned away to hide the tears in her eyes.

Cesare coughed to clear his throat and Elisa realised he was holding back tears too.

'I didn't expect you would have decided to stay here on your own, it's a

lace for just one person. Are you
it's a good idea?' he said, concern
...ving in his eyes.

'Well, we only have fifty empty guest
rooms plus my grandfather's apart-
ments plus the empty staff rooms, plus
the dining-room, the bar, the pool area
but I'm sure I'll be fine.' The enormity
of the emptiness of the hotel was just
dawning on her. 'Maybe it's not such a
good idea.' She tried a wobbly smile as
her eyes filled with tears. 'I've never
been in the hotel when it was empty. I
guess I didn't think this through very
well.'

'Hey, hey, I'm not here to frighten
you.' Cesare pulled her into his arms to
comfort her.

The feel of his strong arms around
her only made her feel more vulnerable
as the scale of her loneliness enveloped
her. She laid her head against his crisp
white shirt and breathed in the smell of
his musky cologne.

Cesare continued holding her as he
spoke.

'It's just as well I came by because there's a car sitting in the car park with two shifty characters in it.'

Elisa jumped, causing them to separate, but Cesare was laughing.

'Sorry, I've done it again. No need to worry, the shifty characters are Stella and Luigi, and they refuse to leave. They say they are prepared to sit up all night in case you need them.'

Elisa clasped her hand over her face as more tears fell at the thought of her grandfather's two loyal and long serving staff, who had known her since she was a child, keeping watch over her.

'I thought I was doing the right thing sending them to their own homes, forgetting that this is as much their home, too. They have an apartment here, but I thought they would welcome the time off.

'It didn't occur to me they would want to be here to make sure all was well. Oh, what wonderful people they are. No wonder my grandfather loved them so much.'

'Come on, Elisa, let's get them indoors. It will make me feel better anyway to know there is someone else with you,' Cesare said in a more serious tone.

'Why? Why would it make you feel better? Asolto isn't in the middle of a huge crime wave that I don't know about, is it?' Elise said in an attempt at light-heartedness.

'Of course not,' he said but Elise detected just a slight hesitation. 'We must always be aware of the opportunist criminal and an empty hotel might just prove too much of a temptation. Let Luigi do what he's good at — he likes to keep the place secure and he won't settle until he's checked it all over.'

Elise smiled. It was true. Luigi was the hotel handyman and night porter and he almost worked around the clock when it was the height of the season but he had done it for as long as she could remember, and together with his wife Stella who was the senior housekeeper they formed a formidable team who kept the hotel running like clockwork.

They had been good and loyal friends to her grandfather and had helped him cope following the death of his beloved wife Rosa five years before.

'Of course they must come in, it was thoughtless of me not to invite them to stay. What must they think of me?' Elisa said.

'They will not think any less of you, Elisa. You are Stephano's granddaughter and they have loved and cared for you since you were a child. They know the pain you carry in your heart — it is their pain, too.' Cesare answered.

'And yours too?' Elisa asked.

'Of course. I was very fond of Stephano. He was a good friend to me.' Cesare lowered his eyes as he spoke and Elisa noticed the charming way his long dark lashes lay across his cheeks.

'Well we'd better get them inside,' she said, gathering herself together, 'or none of us will get any rest.' Together they moved towards the doors and

Cesare indicated towards the car parked in the driveway, as Elisa waited to welcome her faithful protectors.

Once Stella and Luigi were back in the hotel, Luigi began checking all was safe and Stella set about cooking a meal for them all. She was aware Elisa had not eaten all day.

'Will you be joining us?' she asked Cesare, as the smell of olive oil and garlic filled the kitchen.

'No, thank you, Stella. Delicious as it smells I must get home — early start in the morning,' he replied. He turned to Elisa. 'I hope to see you around, then — but not in any professional capacity.' He smiled.

'I'm not sure what my plans are,' she started to say then realised he might think she thought he was hinting at a date.

'I'm probably heading home once the hotel's sorted,' she quickly blustered. 'Unless of course that crime wave hits,' she weakly tried to joke.

'Oh, you're not staying?' He seemed

surprised. 'I just assumed . . . well, I won't keep you back any longer. It must have been a long day for you. Goodnight and again I'm sorry about your grandfather.' He kissed her on both cheeks.

Surprise News

Elisa spent a sleepless night. Despite her reassurance that Stella and Luigi were nearby, she couldn't settle. She felt bereft and abandoned. She dreaded her meeting with her grandfather's solicitor who had asked to see her the next day.

She wondered how her grandfather's estate would be divided. It was something they hadn't discussed other than he once told her that her father's share would be passed to her.

He told her when her father and mother died their estate was put into a trust for her. It paid for her education at university in England and helped her set up her home there.

Elisa enjoyed university so much and had fallen into her post as a result of her placements with the national chain of hotels where she was currently employed.

She had worked hard and climbed the ladder to become assistant manager. Now her career and friends and, of course, until recently a boyfriend, were in England.

Her heart ached at Michael's betrayal and her own foolishness. Etched in her memory was the scene she had encountered on the last day she saw him and the calculating look on the face of that woman.

Elisa welcomed Fiona's offer to come to Italy to support her. They were best friends having attended university together and they now worked together.

Fiona had asked Elisa to be her bridesmaid and then Ava's godmother. Elisa could not contemplate not having them in her life, and she knew Fiona's presence here would help her come to terms with her loss, and the decisions she now had to face.

The experience Elisa had gained growing up with her grandparents had been to her advantage in her chosen career, but their hotel was nothing compared to the 300-room hotels she now helped to manage in England.

She never knew her mother's parents, who were from England, but who had died prior to her parents' marriage. She had thought living there would make her feel closer to her mother but that had never really happened as she had no relatives to help her get to know who her mother had been as a young girl.

Her thoughts also wandered to Cesare. She had been surprised to see him and a little shocked at his profession given the rogue that he was as a child. She smiled at the memories of her schooldays. They had shared happy times as children. Times she had almost forgotten about.

She smiled at the memory of the younger Cesare, awkward in his own body but now he had grown into a very handsome man. She wondered if he was married, or engaged. It hadn't occurred to her to ask. He didn't wear a ring on his wedding finger, she had noticed that. She wondered what he thought of her. She wasn't sure she had left a good impression. He most likely thought she was rude and ungrateful.

⋆　⋆　⋆

As Elisa sat in the solicitor's office she couldn't quite take in all she was hearing. The solicitor, Signor Ricci, a plump, kindly middle-aged man explained it again.

'Your grandfather has left the Hotel Perlino to you, plus a substantial amount of savings. He has instructed a few individual payments be made to loyal members of staff, and a sum to be donated to the local council to continue his charity work.

'There is no debt on the hotel — your grandfather was a very careful man and ensured that he paid every-thing in advance. The hotel can continue to trade, which I am sure is a big relief to you. Once I have settled his estate and having met with your grandfather the week prior to his passing, I am sure there are no monies owed that we do not know of. Even his funeral was settled in advance.' He reached out and touched Elisa gently on the arm.

Elisa struggled to hold back the tears. She had been fearful of what she would hear in the solicitor's office. Her expectation was to be told the hotel still had an outstanding mortgage, given the upgrading her grandfather instructed over the years, and with no-one to share the financial burden with him.

Elisa had anticipated the prospect of selling off the hotel to pay the mortgage and that the staff would lose their jobs.

'You have no idea what a relief that is to hear, Signor Ricci. I have been so worried about breaking bad news to the staff. At least we can continue to trade until . . . '

'Until?' Signor Ricci asked.

'Until I have decided what I am going to do with my own future,' Elisa answered.

'Ah, I see. Well, that's not all I have to tell you, and maybe this piece of news will help you with your decision,' Signor Ricci continued. 'I don't know your grandfather's reasons for doing this, but you inherited an amount from your mother, which your grandfather placed in trust for you with instruction for it to be released either on your wedding day, your thirty-fifth birthday or his death — whichever came first. Did he not mention this to you?'

'No.' Elisa shook her head. 'I have no idea about this or why he made such arrangements.'

'I feel, Elisa, that he wanted you to do as he did and prove that you could make your own way in the world. He was a hard worker, as you know. Maybe he needed you to have that work ethic.'

'My mother was thirty-five when she died. I think he knew I would be all alone in the world someday. Maybe he needed to know I would survive by my own efforts.' Elisa dabbed at her eyes.

'Whatever his reason he invested well

for you, and by today's values those investments are just short of one million euro.'

Elisa gasped.

'Are you sure, Signor Ricci? There couldn't be some mistake?'

'No, Elisa, I'm quite sure. There's a copy of your English grandparents' will here with your family papers showing the split between your mother and your uncle.'

'No, Signor Ricci, now I know there is definitely a mistake. I don't have an uncle. My mother was an only child.'

Signor Ricci adjusted his spectacles, and consulted the paperwork in front of him.

'Look, Elisa, here it is. Your uncle is a Mr John Sinclair and there is an address for him. He would have been thirty-eight then.'

* * *

Elisa arrived back at the hotel to face the worried faces of Stella and Luigi.

Over coffee and pastries, she was able to tell them about the gift Stephano had left them, at which they both exclaimed their thanks for the pleasure of having shared his friendship, and that they needed no reward.

Once Elisa explained to them it was her grandfather's wishes and they must accept it they both sobbed at their friend's thoughtfulness. Elisa took pleasure in reassuring them the hotel could open again, whenever they were ready, and that they could honour all their bookings for the season.

'That is wonderful news and what your grandfather would have wanted. He prided himself on giving service to his guests — especially those who return year after year. He was loyal to his customers, as they were to him,' Stella said.

'Would you like me to contact the staff to tell them to return today?' Luigi asked, eager to be helpful.

'Yes, please, Luigi, but maybe we can ask them to come back tomorrow. That would be time enough and we can start welcoming guests back the day after.' She smiled at Luigi. 'Maybe tonight it can just be the three of us.'

Elisa almost suffocated in the hug Stella and Luigi wrapped her in as they exclaimed their love for her and Stephano.

Elisa had decided on the drive back from the solicitor that she would request a six-month leave of absence from her job, to allow her to see out the busy summer season at Hotel Perlino. She hoped it would give her time to decide what she would do. She needed time to think this through.

As good as the staff were at the hotel and she trusted them all just as her grandfather had done, she didn't see how she could keep on the hotel whilst still living in England. It wouldn't be fair to anyone.

That evening Stella, of course, made a huge meal for them, which Elisa wasn't sure she had the appetite for. Despite the delicious aroma coming from the mushroom risotto, her head was whirling from all she had learned at Signor Ricci's office.

'Stella,' she asked the older woman, 'did my mother or grandparents ever mention that I had an uncle?'

Stella and Luigi both looked puzzled.

'No, my little potato.' Stella fell into the childhood name she called Elisa, which she called all her own children and grandchildren. 'I have never heard of an uncle. Surely if such a person existed he would have come looking for you a long time ago.' She smiled. 'But a certain man did come looking for you today.'

Elisa furrowed her brow, concerned as to who it might be.

'Who was looking for me?'

'The *ispetorre*.'

'Cesare? What did he want? Is something wrong?' Elisa was immediately anxious.

'I don't think so, maybe just amore. He's a single man, married to his job. He needs a good woman.' Stella laughed.

'Not interested.' Elisa kissed her on the cheek. 'Not interested.' Although a part of her was delighted to hear he was single.

Childhood Memories

'Good morning. Welcome to the Hotel Perlino,' Elisa greeted another group of guests to the hotel.

Six weeks had passed since her grandfather's funeral. The hotel was back to running in an efficient style. Elisa took comfort to find some visitors saddened that Stephano had passed away, but uplifted to find positive feedback from guests on the service provided.

It was a double-edged sword. She was determined standards would not slip and guests would not notice any change in the high level of service provided, but at the same time she wanted Stephano to be missed.

'If there is anything we can do to make your stay more comfortable please just ask. The reception is manned twenty-four hours,' Elisa continued.

Since Fiona and Ava's arrival a few days previously Elisa was overjoyed to watch Ava delight in the hotel and the village. She was reminded of her own enjoyment when she lived here as a child when every day brought a new adventure and new people to meet.

It was ideal for children. There were plenty of open park areas, sandy coves on the lakeside and of course the fascination of watching the ferries arrive and depart from the pier, bringing and taking visitors on a regular basis.

With the guests escorted to their rooms by Luigi and his staff, Elisa took a welcome break for a coffee with Fiona.

'I've always loved this hotel, Elisa, especially when you brought me here when we were both starving university students. It has an atmosphere of warmth and love. I never understood how you could bear to leave it.' Fiona sipped her coffee and watched as six-year-old Ava made friends with a little French girl.

'She reminds me of myself at that age,' Elisa said. 'The hotel was like a big playground to me when I visited with my parents and every day brought new playmates.'

'You must miss them all.' Fiona reached for her friend's hand.

'I sometimes struggle to remember my parents but I miss my grandparents. I guess I never really appreciated how much they did for me and their sacrifice to bring me up. I think I was quite awful as a teenager.' She laughed.

'I've got that to look forward to.' Fiona pulled a face in Ava's direction.

'How about Joe? Are you sure he doesn't mind that you and Ava are here?'

'Not at all, he's enjoying the peace and quiet to get some work done.' Fiona laughed at the mention of her husband.

'How is his job doing? I've been so wrapped up in my own issues I never even asked. Last time we spoke he was concerned about a take-over,' Elisa said.

'I think that has been shelved for the moment, but it means longer hours for him, and he misses seeing Ava, and she him.' Fiona made a face. 'But what else can we do? At least he has a job and me too. Anyway, speaking of family, have you done anything about your mysterious uncle?'

'My head's been in a spin with everything that's happened. Cesare offered to make some enquiries with friends he has in the police force in England but to be honest it's not my priority. I can only guess my uncle had good reason not to contact me all those years ago.'

'But it hurts.' Fiona touched Elisa's hand.

'Yes, Fiona, it does. How could he ignore a child, his own flesh and blood who had been orphaned?'

'I don't know, Elisa. Anyway,' Fiona said, changing the subject again, 'Cesare . . . now there is a handsome man. How come you never introduced us when I was young and single?'

'Fiona, I'm shocked!' Elisa laughed, but Fiona spotted the slight blush that moved up her face.

'Cesare, Cesare!' Ava shouted, her little hand waving.

Both women turned to look in the direction Ava was waving, hoping that the subject of their conversation had been out of earshot.

'Good morning, ladies, I trust you are both well,' Cesare said, smiling. 'And how is my little friend today?' he asked Ava as she launched herself at him. 'Making new friends, are you? Well done, we'll soon have you speaking as many languages as your clever god-mother.' He nodded to Elisa as Ava ran off again to play with her friend.

'Would you like some coffee or a cold drink?' Elisa asked, suddenly flustered at Cesare's compliment.

'Yes, please. Perhaps an espresso, if it's no trouble?' Cesare answered.

'I'll get it.' Fiona jumped up. 'That's

if you don't mind keeping an eye on Miss Ava,' and she was gone before they could answer.

'So, I have some news for you regarding your uncle,' he announced to Elisa, looking at her from under his long dark eyelashes.

'Am I going to like this news?' she asked.

'Perhaps not. Your uncle has been in prison,' Cesare replied without further hesitation.

Elise gasped.

'Oh, I didn't expect that. Is that why he didn't contact me, do you think?'

'Not quite. He has been in and out of prison. He seems to favour trying to defraud people or companies.'

'Oh, goodness! I feel so ashamed.'

'Why should you feel ashamed?' Cesare asked, just as Fiona returned with a tray of coffee for them all.

'Who feels ashamed?' she asked.

'Me,' Elisa answered sullenly. 'Turns out my uncle is a cheap fraudster. How lucky am I to find the only family I have

58

left in the world and he's a criminal? No wonder my nonno never told me about him.' As she spoke her voice wobbled.

'I'm sorry I've upset you.' Cesare's brown eyes were full of concern as he looked earnestly at her.

'I think I've heard enough for the moment. If you'll excuse me I must get on with some work now. Fiona, I'll catch up with you later. I hope you and Ava enjoy your day.' Elisa nodded to Cesare who had stood up.

'Thank you, Cesare, I do appreciate that you have worked hard trying to help but let's just call a halt now.' With that she returned into the hotel office.

Cesare made to move to follow her but Fiona stopped him.

'Leave it for just now, Cesare, she needs to take it all in. She's had one blow after another recently. First, she finds her boyfriend cheating on her with another woman, then her grandfather dies, then she has this place to run and now a criminal uncle. It's too much

for anyone but she is strong and she'll
bounce back, you'll see.'

Unwelcome Guests

As Fiona collected Ava and went looking for Elisa, Cesare left and made his way to his car parked nearby, recollecting Fiona's words as he walked — especially the bit about Elisa finding her boyfriend with another woman.

Stephano had mentioned Elisa's boyfriend during their conversations. Cesare assumed work had prevented the boyfriend's presence here to comfort and assist Elisa during this crisis, and for some unknown reason Cesare hadn't been able to bring himself to ask her about him. Now he understood.

Opening the car door, he realised he was incensed that some man could have done this to her. He could not begin to comprehend the hurt she must have suffered and to then face the loss of her grandfather, too.

Of course, he had then stomped in

with his big feet to add to her distress with this news of her uncle. In effect, he knew he had been trying to impress her, which made his blunder even more indefensible.

Fiona was right. This uncle would be of no comfort to Elisa. For the time being, he would continue his enquiries and keep the other piece of information which had been uncovered until Elisa recovered enough to give it consideration. Starting the engine, he headed back to the station. He had work to do.

* * *

Despite Fiona's protests, Elisa encouraged Fiona and Ava to go off to the market in the nearby village, which she knew had a funfair which Ava would enjoy.

She kept herself busy in the office. Bookings were up and the hotel was still making enough money to continue in business. She recognised that the staff were concerned about their jobs and ultimately their futures.

Signor Ricci accompanied her to meet her grandfather's bank manager a few days after their first meeting. She had faith these two men who had served her grandfather well, could be trusted to assist her in making the correct decisions for her and the hotel.

It was all still an enormous strain and she would have dearly loved to have had someone to share the burden. Just having another person to turn to in the night to seek comfort from, would have helped ease the stress.

It wasn't to be, though. Michael had proved to be untrustworthy, a weak man. She was thankful that her grandfather hadn't known of his deception and the hurt he inflicted on her.

Her nonno had been looking forward to meeting Michael for the first time. He had often teased her that she never brought any boys home to meet him.

In truth, Michael had been the only serious boyfriend she ever had. Elisa didn't have time for boyfriends when she worked hard learning her trade and building her career.

With a start, she realised the last long-term friendship she had with a male had been with Cesare, and now she couldn't remember how they had drifted apart.

They were like polite strangers now with a shared history but no real connection.

Elisa realised Cesare, with his good looks, would be popular with women of all ages, so why was he still single? Was he, like her, caught up in his work to the detriment of everything else, and did he see her as part of his work — an incident to be wrapped up and signed off?

She slumped at her desk. Events of the last few weeks had exhausted her and she was grateful for the dedication of Stella and Luigi, who had stepped in to assist in the running of the hotel, and she also appreciated the wonderful staff her grandfather had employed.

Not only did they look after the hotel

but they cared for her, making sure she at least tried to eat and sleep and giving her so much love and support she would never be able to reciprocate.

The arrival of Fiona and Ava had been a much-needed boost. She trusted Fiona and was able to unload all her news, fears and worries, confident in her friend's loyalty and discretion.

Always in the background, too, was Cesare with his uninvited help. Stella had unwittingly given him the information that Elisa had been questioning the existence of an uncle which had led to the bombshell he had just dropped on her today.

Sometimes the past was best left in the past, and she was thankful now that on Signor Ricci's advice she had written a will ensuring that her missing uncle would not inherit from her.

It wasn't a decision she was proud of but he had abandoned her, and now she knew why, she needed to ensure that her grandfather's legacy was protected.

Signor Ricci's experience proved invaluable to her in those early days of coming to terms with the change in her circumstances. His friendship with her grandfather, and his knowledge of how Stephano built the business and to a certain extent his hopes and dreams for Elisa, ensured that he took on the role of protector if only from a legal point of view.

On learning of her break-up with Michael, Signor Ricci wrote to her solicitor in England commencing negotiations on the sale of their flat. It had all seemed hasty and unnecessary to Elisa. However, she lacked the energy to disagree.

Next door to Signor Ricci's office was an estate agent, which specialised in the holiday home market. They had a new employee from England working with them to meet the demand for Italian properties as second homes for Brits.

Signor Ricci introduced him to Elisa as William and she welcomed his help contacting a surveyor in England for a valuation of her flat.

William was charming, and keen to assist her in any way he could. In retrospect, putting the flat on the market was the correct thing to do as her conversation with Fiona indicated she had indeed already closed the door on her relationship with Michael.

There really was no going back as far as she was concerned. She recognised Michael would not have been of any help to her with the events of the last few weeks, and she was honest enough to know she would not have told him all of the provisions of her grandfather's will.

There would have been no trust in their relationship — he had killed it with his affair.

Whether her future lay in Italy or back in England was a decision she still had to face, but it would be without Michael being part of her future.

If Signor Ricci was her legal protector, then Cesare had set himself up as her personal protector with or without her permission. She welcomed his help, and his stories of Stephano always made her laugh. They brought her memories of her grandfather back to life and she could feel his presence and hear his voice throughout the hotel.

This news about her uncle had really shaken her though, more than she thought it could. If only she had someone who could explain to her what had gone wrong in the family.

There was a strange disparity between the person that her mother was and the person that her uncle had become.

Could she open herself up to Cesare to help her further with this? She wasn't sure. Part of her longed for the easy friendship of their youth. The younger Elisa would have told him everything that troubled her.

Her train of thought was interrupted by Jinni the receptionist who popped her head around the office door to warn her there was a coachload of guests arriving from the airport.

Elisa laughed. Although Jinni was more than capable of managing a coachload of guests Elisa liked to follow her grandfather's tradition and greet guests when she could. The hotel was his home and his ethos was you always welcome guests personally into your home.

Still smiling, Elisa entered the reception area where a group of around ten people stood surrounded by various pieces of colourful luggage. As she began her welcome, the smile froze on her face and her throat dried up.

Amongst the new arrivals were two faces she recognised — Michael and the woman whom she had found in her bed.

Two Weeks Too Long

Michael's face also registered shock, and he shuffled nervously, but the woman seemed quite cool, as though this was a normal set of circumstances.

Elisa quickly regained her composure. She was professional and carried out her duties as though nothing was unusual although inwardly she was kicking herself she had not checked the guest list for the day, as she would have spotted his name, and been prepared.

As Michael and his companion reached the desk, Elisa made sure that Jinni checked them in whilst she attended to a family. She fussing over their children, making it difficult for Michael to catch her eye, although she was aware he was watching her.

Once the new guests had been checked in Elisa and Jinni settled down to process the paperwork and passports.

Elisa read that the female with Michael was named Lauren Bradley.

Why they had turned up at her hotel was another issue altogether. Maybe it was to do with the flat but she sensed that Michael had seemed genuinely surprised to see her. She noted they were staying for two weeks. It was going to be a long two weeks and she would need to keep her wits about her as she had no idea what they might be up to.

It was a great relief to Elisa when Fiona and Ava returned and she could tell her about the surprise guests.

'I suppose they could just have booked not knowing it was your hotel. After all, Michael has never been here.' Fiona stirred her coffee as she tried to reassure her friend as Elise explained the arrival of her ex and his new girlfriend during a break from reception.

'I dare say you're right, Fiona, maybe I'm being paranoid but you have to agree that of all the places to come to on holiday, why choose Italy when he knows I'm here?' Elisa said in a puzzled voice.

'It does seem strange, but maybe she booked it without him knowing where he was going. Maybe he just agreed to a holiday.'

'Well, he seems to have got over me fast enough to be able to come for a holiday. I wonder when they booked. It still seems a strange coincidence to me.' Elisa tapped her foot against the table leg as she watched the barman prepare a cocktail using brightly coloured paper flowers as an embellishment, much to the guest's amusement.

'Try not to dwell on it. Hopefully they will keep a low profile, for everyone's sake.' Fiona nodded in Ava's direction, who was playing with her new bat and ball as Luigi counted in Italian with her.

'Oh, of course. Ava knows Michael. She won't understand what's going on.' Elisa shook her head. 'This is all such a mess.'

'Yes, but it's not you who made the

mess and I'm still going to be here during their stay, moral support and all that.' Fiona playfully punched Elisa on the arm.

'Thank you, Fiona. I don't know how I could have coped without you.'

'Oh, I think maybe a certain handsome inspector would have helped.' Fiona laughed.

'Don't even think that!' Elisa answered but she smiled as she spoke.

'Why not? He's a lovely man. Why have you never mentioned him in your tales of growing up here?' Fiona asked.

'I don't know. We were friends when we were young, always having adventures. It's that kind of place here. There was always something to do as a child and everyone knew us so although we were mischievous we weren't bad children.

'I suppose when we reached that awkward teenage stage we just drifted apart,' Elisa said.

'I was busy with my schoolbooks. I was determined to study in England.

When I moved to England, we didn't keep in touch. Then we were grown up and moving on with our lives. I didn't recognise him at the airport.

'He is quite handsome though, isn't he? I wonder why he hasn't been snapped up by a gorgeous Italian signorina?'

Elisa felt her face flush as she spoke.

'What am I saying!' She laughed. 'I don't have the time or energy to be involved in anything remotely romantic. I know nothing about him now — we haven't spoken for years. And yet Stephano kept up a friendship with him. That pleases me in some way I can't explain.'

Fiona raised her eyebrow.

'Hmm.'

'Oh, you!' Elisa threw a cushion at her friend. Ava jumped between the two women, giggling at them, desperate to join in the fun. 'It's good to have you both here,' Elisa said, cuddling them both. 'You're keeping me sane.'

Perfect Timing

Cesare could not settle during the day. Elisa's face at the disappointing news of her uncle had upset him and he was sorry to have been the cause. He needed to see her to make sure she was OK.

He was disappointed in himself. He had promised his old friend he would look after Elisa, and so far he seemed to have always been the bearer of bad news.

It upset him, too, that her loss of Stephano had followed the betrayal of her boyfriend. He understood her hurt and confusion and would do anything to help her, if she would let him.

Now evening was falling he decided he needed to see her again to try to put right his earlier clumsy behaviour.

His timing was perfect. As he arrived at the hotel, Fiona and Ava had gone to bed exhausted with their busy day, and Elisa was handing over to Luigi for the late shift as he walked into reception.

Cesare and Luigi greeted each other and then Elisa welcomed him with a kiss on each cheek.

'Have you eaten, Cesare? I was just about to have something.'

As they shared a late meal cooked for them by the hotel chef, Cesare felt relieved that Elisa seemed to have recovered from the news about her uncle. He was less than pleased when she told him about her unwelcome guests.

'Would Michael have known where the hotel was even though he hadn't been here?' he asked, annoyed that this man had come back into her life after what he had done to her.

'I doubt it. He never took much notice when I spoke of it.' Elisa recollected Michael never asked about her grandfather or her family, and because of that she never really shared much information about it with him.

'Also I removed all my belongings from the flat before I came over here. Most of it is in storage at Fiona's until I decide what I'm doing. Of course, William will have written to Michael regarding the sale of the flat, but I don't think he would have given my current address.'

'Who is William?' Cesare said, his brow furrowing.

For no reason, Elisa could feel herself blush under his scrutiny as she explained he worked with Signor Ricci.

'And he is English, this William?'

'Yes.'

'I'm sorry that I upset you earlier,' Cesare said suddenly.

'You weren't to know what impact the news would have.' Elisa kept her head down as she spoke.

'It was still wrong of me — a professional hazard.' Cesare bowed his head. Then changing the subject back to Michael he frowned. 'I am intrigued about this person he is with . . . Lauren, you called her? Do you have a copy of her passport number still on file?' Cesare asked.

'Of course, but you don't have any reason for me to pass it over to you.' She smiled at him.

'Ah, always the professional. At least reassure me you have warned staff to be on the alert. This may be a coincidence but you never know — there are some strange people in this world.'

'Yes, well, without giving too much of an explanation, I have mentioned they may be the type of vexatious complainers that hotels sometimes get,' she said.

'Have you met her before?' Cesare asked, noting the shadow that had fallen across Elisa's eyes as she spoke of Michael, and being aware of the information Fiona had already given him.

He was interested to see if she would trust him enough to share with him how she and Lauren had met.

'Not exactly met. I found them together.' Elisa held Cesare's gaze as she spoke and waited for the penny to drop.

'Together, oh . . . together.' Cesare's eyes widened in realisation, both at the situation but also at Elisa's honesty. 'How distressing for you, and how strange they should turn up here. I would have thought this would have been the last place they would want to spend a holiday.' He shook his head.

'It upsets me you have another worry to deal with,' he added. 'I've enjoyed watching you begin to glow with health now that you are home. The sun, the air and the good food and wine were beginning to fill out the hollows in your face and put a shine back in your eyes.'

'You mean I'm getting fat?' Elisa said in mock indignation, pleased to move to another subject.

'I've done it again, haven't I? Big boots right in.'

'Yes, and what do you mean by home? Is this my home?' she asked.

'I hope so. I'm so pleased to have you here. I didn't realise how much I missed our friendship.' He reached over and ran his fingers over her hand.

She let it linger.

'Time is moving on. I have until autumn to decide if I'm returning to my job back in England.'

'Or?' he questioned.

'Or stay here and take on my grandfather's legacy, and leave my life and career in England.'

'Your grandfather would not have wanted you to take over the hotel reluctantly.'

She snatched back her hand in confusion at his directness.

'You seem to know a lot about my grandfather's wishes.'

Cesare sighed.

'Another apology, Elisa, I should not presume to speak about your grandfather's wishes, however well I knew him and valued his friendship. I don't mean to hurt you when I speak of him . . . '

'How did you know my grandfather so well?' Elisa softened her tone. 'I've never understood how you came to be such friends after we had grown up and moved away.'

'Ah, it is a long story of a man who was wise enough to see a young boy on the verge of making a mess of his life and who was caring enough to set him on the right path.' He stared into the distance as he reminisced.

'You? Were you that young boy?'

'Ha! No, but I was the young trainee police officer who was run ragged by the escapades of the boy, and believe me he had a lot of energy and an active imagination.

'His father was an alcoholic and his mother couldn't cope so he was running wild. One night he broke into the hotel and I found him stealing food from the kitchen.'

'So he was hungry? How sad. Poor child.'

'Yes, he was fourteen and the eldest in his family. He was only trying to feed his younger brother and sister. His exploits were frustrating the enthusiastic officer in me. He made it hard for me to help him.'

Elisa shook her head at the thought of the boy trying to provide for his family. Cesare saw the concern in her eyes and it touched him.

'What happened to him?' she asked. 'Did you arrest him?'

'Well, he was leaving me no option but to arrest him with his mischief but your grandfather asked if he could speak to the boy and he sat with him that night and asked him where he saw himself in ten years' time.'

Elisa smiled.

'That sounds so like him.'

'Of course, the young boy given his background could not answer him, he couldn't visualise that far into the future, he was living day to day.'

'Poor soul,' Elisa said.

'Yes, but your grandfather made a deal with the boy. If he agreed to come and help in the hotel after school and in the holidays for a small wage and left-overs to help feed his family, then he would not press charges.'

'I didn't know any of this. Why don't I know this?'

'Well, you were probably at university at the time.'

'And wrapped up in my own world.'

'I didn't say that, Elisa.' He patted her hand as he spoke.

Elisa felt the tension leave her body again as she realised Cesare wasn't judging her.

'When we are young we don't always see the whole picture. I certainly didn't. I just wanted the boy to stop misbehaving. Your grandfather made the connection that the boy needed to work and could then take pride in his efforts of providing for his family, instead of acquiring a criminal record that would help no-one,' Cesare said.

'He was that kind of man, your grandfather. He could see the bigger picture long before most people could.'

'Indeed he could — that was how he built a successful business.' Elisa smiled. 'What happened to the boy? Did he agree to the deal?'

'Of course he did. He was poor but he wasn't stupid. The alternative would not have been too good for him. He enjoyed working at the hotel and learned a lot, and when he left school he went to college to study cookery, assisted by a loan from your grandfather, which he agreed to work off when he qualified.'

'Did it work out for him? Did he qualify, do you know where he ended up?' Elisa was engrossed in the story of the boy her grandfather had helped.

'One question at a time.' Cesare laughed at her childlike enthusiasm to know the answer.

'It did, and I sure know it worked out well — he's a fabulous chef.' As Cesare spoke he pushed his plate away in appreciation.

'Really good.' His eyes twinkled.

Elisa looked at him, her eyes opening wider as the realisation set in.

'Do you mean Roberto, our chef, is he the boy you're speaking of?'

'Yup,' Cesare smiled, 'and I spent a

lot of time here making sure he behaved, and his younger brother and sister whom you also know.'

'I do?'

Cesare laughed, enjoying himself in her company.

'I won't keep you guessing. Jinni is Roberto's sister. Your grandfather also employed Jinni and Paulo, the other brother, to help when they were old enough.'

'We don't have a Paulo on the staff,' Elisa said, puzzled.

'Ah, Paulo, well, he is another story for another day.' Cesare shrugged his shoulders. 'I think it's fair to say that your grandfather saved Roberto and his family from poverty, and of course Roberto repaid the loan long ago but chose to stay here. They all helped keep an eye on your grandfather, for they owed him so much,' Cesare said.

'Then of course came the day that your grandfather had the 'Where do you see yourself in ten years' time?' conversation with me,' he continued.

'He made me think of my future and he was the reason I ended up training in Rome to become an inspector.'

'I can't believe I didn't know all this. I owe you an apology — you really did have a strong friendship with my nonno,' Elisa said.

'I wouldn't lie to you, Elisa.' Cesare held her gaze. 'He had a big influence on my life. And as you know he was a much loved and respected man. There are families all over this village who owe him a debt for the kindness he showed them in times of trouble.

'I think he knew such sadness in his life that he recognised it in others.' Cesare played awkwardly with his wine glass as he spoke.

'You, Cesare — did you know such sadness?' Elisa reached out towards him. Her touch burned into his soul and he was pleased when Fiona and Ava appeared, and interrupted the moment.

Ava skipped happily towards Elisa.

'I want to feed the ducks and swans.

They're very hungry,' Ava lisped in her childish voice.

'Do you, honey? That's kind of you but they will be all tucked up for the night now.' Elisa swept her god-daughter on to her knee and smothered her in kisses.

'I fear she's had a nap and she's full of energy again,' Fiona said.

At that moment Michael and Lauren passed through the terraced area on their way out of the hotel. Ava jumped up.

'Look, Mummy it's Michael!

'Michael, Michael!' she began to call.

A Nasty Piece of Work

Elisa froze. Michael stopped in his tracks and moved towards Ava just as Fiona intercepted.

'Let's not disturb Michael and his new friend. I think they're going out.' She bent down and began to turn Ava away from Michael.

Lauren spoke.

'Michael, are you not going to introduce me to your sweet little friend?' She began to walk towards Ava, who was now beginning to twist out of her mother's grasp.

Before anyone else could react, Cesare was on his feet and placed himself between Ava and Lauren. Ava, startled by Cesare's speed, turned back to her mother who scooped her up and held her in her arms.

'I don't think he is, are you?' Cesare faced Michael, whilst the position of his body blocked Lauren from moving towards Ava. 'I think you are both about to turn and leave the terrace, aren't you, Michael?' Cesare said in a low controlled voice.

Lauren seemed unperturbed.

'What business is it of yours?'

But Michael, aware they were beginning to attract attention from other guests, and unsure who this tall, striking Italian man was, took her by the arm and led her towards the driveway and out of the hotel grounds.

'Come on, Ava, let's get you a hot chocolate and then it's time for bed,' Fiona said, taking Ava's hand. 'I'll try to explain it to her,' she whispered to Elisa.

'I'm sorry, Fiona, I really am,' Elisa said.

'Hey, it's not your fault but that Lauren is a piece of work, isn't she?' Fiona rolled her eyes as she spoke. 'Thank you so much, Cesare, that was more than a bit awkward. Goodnight, you guys, play nice, no falling out.'

She kissed both Elisa and Cesare and headed to her room with Ava skipping beside her, all thought of the last few minutes gone as she anticipated a cup of hot chocolate.

'Now will you let me see their passports?' Cesare inclined his head to one side as he asked Elisa.

'No. Yes, she is an unpleasant person but that's not a crime.' Elisa smiled. 'Thank you, though, for what you did. Hopefully they've got the message to stay clear of Fiona and Ava.'

'You're welcome. If they give you any trouble, phone me.'

'I will. Now I need to get some rest, as do you. We're not holidaymakers. I need to work early tomorrow morning,' Elisa said kissing him on both cheeks. 'Good night, Cesare.'

'Good night, Elisa.' Cesare held her delicate face in his and gently kissed her forehead.

Elisa watched as he walked towards his car. She could still feel the soft touch of his lips on her skin, and her feelings confused her.

She wasn't sure she could trust anyone in that way again, but Cesare tore at her heart. She wasn't strong enough to deal with these emotions at the moment. She turned and made her way back to her apartment.

★ ★ ★

Cesare sat in his car, his whole body shaking. He wanted so much to embrace her, and never let her go again. To protect her from this world. But he knew she was vulnerable and he would never take advantage of that vulnerability. She needed time and he was prepared to wait.

From her vantage point of a nearby bar, where she and Michael stopped for a drink, Lauren watched, displeased at what she had just witnessed on the terrace of Hotel Perlino. She dispatched Michael to find the cocktail menu as she dialled a number on her mobile.

She tapped her long, polished fingernails off the table as it rang out. At last the person on the other end answered.

'William,' she said, 'I think we have a problem.'

Precious Friendship

Cesare let himself into his apartment on the outskirts of the village. He poured himself a glass of wine and opened the doors on to the balcony.

He sat and gazed over the dark expanse of the lake and ran his fingers through his unruly hair. He remembered the winter nights when the tourist season was over and he and Stephano spent time playing chess and putting the world to rights.

Stephano had spoken of Elisa whom Cesare knew from their schooldays and Cesare remembered the awkwardness of them as teenagers when they realised that childhood had passed.

Cesare might have asked her for a date but not only was he unable to pluck up the courage but he somehow sensed that he could never hold on to her.

Elisa was ambitious to get good grades and study in England and he encouraged her to achieve her ambition.

Cesare was clever, too, but less focused on the future — that came later with Stephano's help. Cesare, with hindsight now, realised Stephano had been worried about his own health and was concerned for Elisa's future. With the arrogance of youth, Cesare reassured him that he would look out for her, never realising what he was promising.

His promise was sincere enough, and he had resources at his fingertips to keep her safe but he hadn't realised that seeing her again would bring back old memories.

Nor had he realised that he couldn't prevent her being hurt and that every hurt and obstacle she was facing would cut him to the core, too.

He traced the outline of the wine glass with his long slender fingers and listened to the echo of cicadas chirping into the night air.

It had been a shock to see her at the airport. He hadn't expected her to look so small and vulnerable. His memories of her were of a self-sufficient and capable girl ready to take on the world. His first instinct was to wrap her up and take all the hurt away.

Life, however, wasn't like that, and he couldn't stop her hurting. In fact recently, to his disappointment he had been the cause of some of her upset. He had felt awkward around her and she him, but he hoped things were beginning to thaw between them.

His friendship with Stephano had been precious to him, and he had been touched when Stephano spoke of leaving him something in his will, which Cesare had refused.

He told his old friend he had no need of anything. Thanks to him he had been set on his own road in life and he needed nothing more from him.

Stephano had nodded acceptance of Cesare's choice, and Cesare wondered if it had been some kind of test, which he had passed with Stephano's approval.

He rattled his pencil against his desk. Elisa had clearly been shaken to see her ex-boyfriend Michael with his new girlfriend. Was it coincidence? Who was this Lauren person?

Elisa was a stickler for the rules but he had other ways of finding things out. Reaching for his phone he made a call asking for yesterday's passenger lists for planes arriving at Verona airport from the UK to be made available to him. One way or another he would get to the bottom of who Lauren was and why she had chosen to come to Hotel Perlino.

*   *   *

Every second week during high season the hotel hosted a gala dinner for hotel guests. The tradition had slipped over the last few weeks, but tonight it was going ahead. Elisa knew the day would become very busy and so she took the opportunity to spend part of the morning with Fiona and Ava.

After breakfast they headed to the swing park before the day became too hot.

As they walked along the lakeside towards the park Elisa and Fiona laughed as Ava waved to her friends, the ducks.

'I know it's only been a few days but I cannot believe how quickly Ava has settled in to life here and the hotel,' Fiona said.

'She reminds me of happier times when I had carefree days along the lakeside and around the hotel.' Elisa smiled as she watched her. 'It was like a giant playground and all the staff were like my family.'

'But what about when you lost your parents? That must have been so hard. I look at Ava and my heart breaks at the very thought of her ever having to cope with such a loss at an early age.'

'It was hard. Everything came crashing in on me, and I was so angry. I became cheeky and out of control for a while.'

'That must have been difficult for your grandparents.'

They reached the park and settled on a bench underneath the shade of the pine trees as Ava played on the roundabout, smiling at a little boy who joined her.

'I'm sure it was but I didn't take their feelings into account. They had lost their daughter and were left with this wilful child and a business to run. It must have been awful for them.

'Only now can I realise how difficult it must have been for them to get through each day. But my grandparents had created Hotel Perlino in a community that supported each other and that's what happened. The community pulled us all through and out the other side of that huge wave of despair.'

Elisa stared out across the lake as the memories flooded in.

'I've lost that and I don't know how it happened. I stayed away too long. I don't know how to make it better and I don't know what is the best thing to do. My nonno has left me financially comfortable. I'm too young to retire and I've worked too hard to give up on my career.'

'A lot of people are depending on your decision, too, Elisa. I'm sure that doesn't help.'

'No, it doesn't, it's extra pressure. I'm trying to make sure I'm doing the right thing for everyone.'

'Well, I'm not covering your shifts for ever.' Fiona punched her friend playfully on the shoulder, lifting the mood. 'I don't have the childcare. Did I tell you my parents are moving house?'

'No, you didn't. I'm so sorry, Fiona, I've been so caught up in my own troubles I forgot about your parents. I'm so selfish. Is your dad moving for work?'

'Don't be silly, you've had loads on your mind. Yep, Dad's been offered a caretaking job. It comes with a small flat but it's quite far out of town so we won't see them as much.'

'Oh, that's a shame. Ava loves spending time with them.'

'Yes. Mum's a bit upset by it, with me being an only child too. Give it time, we'll all adjust. I just don't want to lose my best friend, too.' Fiona made a silly face that made Elisa laugh and they both dissolved into giggles.

Ava came running towards them.

'What are you laughing at, Auntie Elisa?'

'Your mummy, Ava, she's being silly. Come on, let me push you on the swing.' Elisa lifted Ava and made her way towards the swings leaving Fiona giggling on the bench.

Let's Get the Party Started!

When they arrived back at the hotel, Fiona and Ava headed to the pool, whilst Elisa joined in with the preparations for the evening.

This was the first gala dinner since the hotel had reopened following Stephano's passing, and Elisa appreciated how hard the staff worked to make sure that it was an enjoyable night for all the guests.

The kitchen was flat out preparing the menu that Stephano had always favoured for such a night, bringing together a wide, varied choice of food from the area, with a few surprises thrown in for fun.

The musicians practised on the terrace and Luigi cleared rogue leaves from the apple and olive trees, whilst muttering to himself under his breath about the wind.

Although the gala was a huge amount of extra work for the staff every two weeks, it was something that guests enjoyed and brought them back year after year. Elisa remembered Stephano explaining to her.

'The hotel is our home and when you have guests to your home you must ensure they feel welcome and special. Our gala dinner is our welcome to our guests and tells them we value you and your custom.

'Some guests will enjoy and never return but others will remember your welcome and they will tell their friends and they will come back, and that is when you know you have done a good job.'

She smiled at the memory and jumped when the phone rang bringing her back to earth.

Elisa was surprised hear William's voice.

'Is everything OK?' she asked,

making a mental note to stop assuming the worst every time the phone rang.

'Just about, although there seems to have been a bit of a hold up with the sale of the flat. Michael isn't responding to the request for a valuation,' he said.

'Well, I might have the answer to that. He's here,' Elisa said, flopping into her seat in the office.

'I don't understand . . . ' William said.

'He's here as a guest at the hotel, with his new girlfriend.'

'You're joking! Cheeky devil.'

Elisa laughed despite the situation.

'That's one way to put it.'

'It's good to hear you laugh,' William said.

Elisa felt her cheeks warm at his remark.

'Do you think I could get him to come into the office whilst he is here to discuss the sale of your flat?' William asked.

'I think you might have a battle on

your hands with his latest flame Lauren.'

'Really? What's she like?'

'We're having a gala dinner tonight at the hotel. Signor Ricci and his wife are coming. Why don't you come, too, then you can judge for yourself?' Elisa said.

'Sounds like fun. Thank you. I'll see you there.'

Elisa had surprised herself by making the invitation to William. Was she inviting him in a professional capacity or did she enjoy his company, although they had barely spoken?

And what about Cesare? How would he react to William's presence at her table? Did Cesare's opinion of William matter to Elisa? She was allowed to have friends. Did she feel guilty that William made her feel light-hearted or was she just feeling homesick? There was that question again. Where was home?

★ ★ ★

The day passed in a whirlwind of activity and before she knew it Elisa was getting into her dress for the evening.

Ava bounced into Elisa's bedroom squeaking with delight.

'Are you ready for the party, Auntie Elisa?'

'Yes, I am, and look at you, my gorgeous girl! You are so pretty in your party dress.' Elisa smiled as Ava danced around the room, her little feet tip-tapping in her party shoes on the tiled floor as she held the skirt of her pink dress making it billow out as she twirled.

Fiona and Ava were staying with Elisa in the apartment which was attached to the hotel, and which had been her home when she had lived with her grandparents. Elisa enjoyed having them to stay. It breathed life into the apartment and Ava's exuberance was catching.

'You are going to be the belle of the ball.' Elisa clasped Ava's hand and they moved into the next room to check on Fiona.

'What does that mean, Auntie Elisa?' Ava said.

'It means you will be the most beautiful girl at the gala.'

'My mummy is beautiful, too.' Ava skipped ahead to where her mother was making last minute adjustments to her make-up. Then having second thoughts she turned back. 'You're beautiful, too, Auntie Elisa.'

Elisa and Fiona agreed wholeheartedly with Ava they were all looking good.

'Well, let's get this party started,' they chorused.

As they walked through the hotel and on to the terraced area an atmosphere of anticipation met them.

Sunset had replaced the overpowering heat of the day, and the cooler evening air proved a welcome delight. The faint scent of lemon balm and jasmine wafted from the gardens.

Pockets of guests had gathered

enjoying pre-dinner drinks. Above them strings of fairy-lights and paper lanterns twinkled amongst the trees. From the small stage area where the musicians were seated the sound of soft music drifted into the night air, drowning out the usual chirp of cicadas.

In a long cotton dress with spaghetti straps, which showed off her sunkissed shoulders, Elisa mingled with guests as she had watched her grandfather do countless times before.

Memories came flooding back and she steadied herself against a chair as she took a deep breath and forced herself to continue keeping a warm smile on her face. She felt like one of Ava's ducks paddling furiously amongst a sea of guests.

Looking around the terrace she couldn't see Cesare and for a moment she could not remember if she had invited him. Doubt sprung up in her. Surely she had. He would know to come, wouldn't he?

At that moment she spotted Michael

and Lauren. She had hoped they wouldn't attend but as they were paying guests they were entitled, and she couldn't really stop them.

Moving back towards her table, which she was pleased the staff had placed far away from Michael and Lauren, Elisa lifted her mobile to phone Cesare, just as Signor and Signora Ricci arrived, accompanied by William.

William was casually dressed in a white linen shirt and dark trousers and the look he gave Elisa showed he was impressed with her appearance.

As Elisa introduced him to Fiona, Stella led the waiting staff out, and invited the guests to take their seats, and the gala commenced.

Wiping a tear from her eye, Elisa smiled at Stella. All this was what made Hotel Perlino, and was the reason guests returned year after year.

A Night to Remember

Cesare sat in his office checking his e-mails for replies in response to his queries about Michael and Lauren, and struggled to make sense of what was implied.

Worse still, he tried to figure how much he could or should say to Elisa. He also sought to figure out his own feelings for Elisa. Despite her vulnerability, Cesare knew she was a resilient woman.

She came from strong stock and he realised once she recovered from recent events she would be more than capable of lifting herself up and getting on with life. He wondered if Stephano sensed that in her.

Cesare stared unseeing at the screen in front of him, as he again asked himself where did he want Elise's new life to be?

As a friend, he wanted her to make the correct decision to take her career and life forward. But as a . . . as a what? Did he want to be more than a friend? Did he want to make that move? Was it too soon, was she still too fragile?

Was *he* still too fragile? He, too, had suffered a broken heart during his time living in Rome, another life event Stephano had helped him deal with. Did his profession cause him to worry she would doubt his intention? Was that really a concern or an excuse? Was he protecting her or himself?

He had unexpressed feelings for her in the past but they had both been too young and needed to experience life.

Now, well — was the time right for them? He had been happy with his life and work until he saw her at the airport and all the old feelings had rushed in, and with them discontentment.

Not for the first time did he wonder how their lives would have been if they had taken different paths when they left school. If Elisa hadn't gone to England would she have been content to stay in Asolto? Would the village have been big enough to contain her quest to fulfil her career?

If Elisa had stayed would they have had a relationship? None of the answers to his questions mattered. They were different people now, both left fragile by betrayal.

At any rate, he believed she needed to know the other information about her uncle, and time was running out. Elisa might return to England at any time.

It had been a long day. He and his men had been out since early morning dealing with an incident, and he wanted to go home and eat but he needed to be sure of his facts. The last thing he needed to do was upset Elisa again.

Calling his sergeant over he asked him to check up on an address that may be part of the jigsaw puzzle he was trying to solve. With the information confirmed, he ran his hand over his face rough with five o'clock shadow, then he set off for Hotel Perlino.

★   ★   ★

'I can't eat any more,' Fiona remarked to Elisa. 'I'm fit to burst and this is only the secondo-course.'

Elisa laughed.

'Yes, which is actually the third course — when Italians have a gala they really enjoy themselves.'

Ava clapped her hands as the magicians performed tricks and made balloon models for the children, and for some of the grown-ups too. The entertainers moved from table to table causing great hilarity as they teased the men and flirted with the ladies.

The musicians performed popular Italian classics ranging from the romantic to children's nursery rhymes.

A roar of approval rose as the kitchen staff led by Roberto carried forth large platters of suckling pig, beef, lamb, sausages, salmon and lobster.

William turned to Elisa.

'I was about to agree with Fiona but I think I might manage a bit more. This is a wonderful spectacle.'

'Please do, and there are still more courses to come. Are you enjoying our gala?' Elisa said.

'Yes, and I'm enjoying the company more,' he answered.

'Good. I am, too,' Elisa said and meant it. William proved to be charming company. He was deferential to Signor and Signora Ricci, courteous to the staff and Fiona and he indulged Ava's questions.

As the meal came to an end, the staff came on to the terrace to take a bow. The guests applauded and shouted, 'Bravo.'

Elisa breathed a sigh of relief. The meal had gone without a hitch and now all that was left was for the guests to enjoy the music and relax. The music started again and some couples including the Riccis took to the floor and showed off their dancing skills.

Mesmerised by the dancers and deafened by the noise of applause, Elisa hadn't noticed Cesare make his way on to the terrace and he was beside her before she could react.

'Buona sera, signorina,' he said stiffly. 'I am sorry to intrude. I can see this is a bad time.' He stared hard at William as he spoke as he noted his arm casually draped across the back of Elisa's chair, before turning his gaze back to Elisa.

Elisa was flustered.

'Cesare, why are you so late? You've missed the meal. Did you get held up with work?' She jumped up almost knocking over a glass.

Cesare caught it before it fell to the ground.

'I apologise. I was unaware the gala evening had been arranged. Perhaps I mislaid my invitation in all my paperwork.'

'This is William,' Elisa blustered, 'he's an estate agent.' She avoided looking at Cesare. His tone had confirmed she had forgotten to invite him, and why did she introduce William as an estate agent rather than explain he was the estate agent acting for her? They had discussed him earlier. Elisa was confused by her own reactions.

William remained seated, his arm remaining in place across the chair, his muscular chest straining against his shirt, as both men nodded an acknowledgement at each other.

Stella appeared with Luigi close behind carrying a coffee for Cesare.

'Shall I arrange some food for you, ispetorre?' she said pointedly. Elisa realised her mistake in not reminding Cesare he was welcome at the gala had been construed as an insult to him.

Before Cesare had a chance to answer, Fiona came running towards them.

'Have you seen Ava?' she asked, panic rising in her voice. 'I can't find her. Where is she? Elisa, I can't see her.' She grabbed Elisa's arm. 'Where is she?'

'Ava, Ava!' she called desperately towards the dancers on the terrace.

Cesare Takes Control

'Fiona, calm down. Tell me what happened?' Cesare took hold of Fiona and made her face towards him.

'I took her to the bathroom to wipe her face and hands but she ran off before I had finished wiping mine. I thought she had come straight back to the table.'

Cesare turned to Luigi.

'Check the swimming pool,' he said in an authoritative voice.

Fiona gasped and covered her mouth with her hand as Luigi ran off towards the pool area, concern etched across his face.

'No! Please no!' she shouted.

Elisa looked at Cesare.

'It's only precautionary,' he soothed Fiona. 'Stella, can you please ask the musicians to stop for a moment and use their microphone to ask if anyone has seen her.'

'Elisa, can you please get Roberto and the bar staff to prevent any cars leaving the car park and to guard the exits, especially the one leading to the main street.' Elisa's mouth started to wobble and her legs felt like lead. 'Hurry, Elisa, please.' Cesare looked straight into her eyes in a look communicating the urgency of the situation to her. It worked and she found the strength to head towards the kitchen issuing instructions to all the staff she met on route.

'Is there anything I can do?' William asked.

'You can stay with Fiona,' Cesare instructed as he reached for his mobile to call for back up.

Just as the music stopped, and Stella began to make the announcement, Roberto spotted Ava walking hand in hand with Lauren through the apple trees.

'There she is!' he shouted. All eyes turned towards the direction Roberto was pointing.

Fiona ran towards her, relief and

terror combined.

'Where have you been, Ava?' Fiona shouted, grabbing her from Lauren and lifting her into her arms. 'What right did you have to take her?' Fiona screamed at Lauren.

'Her balloons got stuck high up in the bushes at the other side of the car park. I was helping her get them down. It took longer than I thought, they are so fragile they can go far in a short time. I'm sure your CCTV can confirm if you check.' Lauren smiled innocently towards Cesare who once again formed a barrier between her and the others.

'I shall check and very carefully. I suggest you keep your distance from the little girl for the remainder of your holiday. I won't make the suggestion again.' Cesare made his intentions clear by the tone of his voice.

'I'm sorry for any trouble we've caused. I'm sure Lauren meant no harm. I hope Ava is OK. I can assure you we'll keep out of your way,' Michael said, taking Lauren by the elbow. Ignoring her attempt at protesting her innocence he led her back towards their table.

Cesare watched as they appeared to row with each other. Michael's anger at Lauren seemed genuine.

Elisa nodded for the music to start up again and instructed the bar staff to give all the guests a glass of prosecco. The incident had only lasted minutes and the guests had barely noticed but Elisa was shaken to the core.

When Lauren had spoken, she didn't address Fiona, she looked straight at Elisa, whilst Michael kept his head lowered. The words sounded sweet enough but what did she mean by they can go far in a short time? Was it a threat?

'Thank you, Cesare,' Fiona said, her face taught with emotion, 'for taking control.' Cesare hugged her and tickled Ava under the chin.

'You gave us all a fright, young lady. Next time you wait for your mama, OK?' he said.

'OK,' Ava said, nodding and yawning at the same time, unaware of the scare she had caused to the adults.

'Yes, that was quite impressive,' William said holding out his hand to Cesare, who strode past his open hand and taking Elisa by the elbow steered her in the direction of the office.

'I realise you are busy just now, with many things . . . ' Cesare said with a slight incline of his head towards the direction they had just come from.

'Cesare, I'm sorry if I forgot to invite you. I thought I had but it would appear not. It wasn't deliberate,' Elisa started to say.

'No matter, it's good to know I wasn't missed.' Cesare could not prevent the hurt tone in his voice. 'Anyway, I need to speak to you in relation to your uncle,' he continued.

'Cesare, I really don't want to know. I managed without knowing he existed all my life I don't see what information you can give me that would be so important,' Elisa answered.

Cesare sighed.

'As you wish, Elisa. I'll leave you to your guests.' He turned towards the door to go. 'Please arrange for Luigi to have the CCTV tape ready for me tomorrow.

'No,' Elisa reached out for his arm, 'don't go, please stay and have a drink and something to eat.'

'I have an early start tomorrow, so no, thank you.' Cesare looked deep into her eyes. '*Arrivederci*, Elisa.' He turned and left.

Elisa flopped into the office chair and laid her head in her hands, hot tears stinging her eyes. She had hurt him, but didn't he see that it hadn't been deliberate? His goodbye had sounded so final. If only she could chase after him to explain she could make him understand it had all been a mistake, but she had guests — she was still working.

She stood up, gave herself a shake and went back on to the terrace, smiling to Signor and Signora Ricci.

'Is the little one OK?' Signora Ricci asked. 'Cesare is a fine man we are very lucky to have him here protecting us. Your grandfather thought so, too.'

Elisa reassured them Ava and Fiona were shaken but otherwise OK.

When the food and music finished, and the staff received a final round of applause, the terrace grew quieter and people retired to their rooms or left to go into town.

The Riccis also left after expressing their enjoyment of the evening. Signora Ricci turned out to be a charming lady who had known Elisa's nonna, and she insisted Elisa visit her at some time soon. Elisa promised her she would.

Elisa noticed that Lauren and Michael were no longer sitting on the terrace and she was thankful they were no longer in her view.

'Would you like to move to another bar or hotel for a change of scene?' William asked Elisa. 'The change might do you good. You seem a bit tense after all that has gone on tonight.'

'I think I would like a walk down near the water if that would be OK?' Elisa agreed. 'I'll just let Fiona and Jinni know where I'm going.'

'Would it be all right for Joe to join us for the last week of our break?' Fiona asked when Elisa entered the apartment.

'Of course, this is as much your home as mine, isn't it, Ava?' She held her god-daughter in a hug, thankful for the happy outcome of Ava's adventure.

She noticed Fiona's face streaked with tears.

'Oh, Fiona, I'm so sorry you've had such a fright. Would you like me to stay here with you and help get Ava ready for bed?'

'No, I'm fine, honestly, just a bit shaken. I can't believe the audacity of that woman. She deliberately tried to frighten us.'

'She's a strange one, for sure,' Elisa agreed.

'Thank heaven Cesare was here,' Fiona said.

'Well I'm not his favourite person at the moment, but I'm very glad he was here and able to take control of the situation. I'm going for a walk with William if you're sure you'll be OK.'

'I would feel better if you were going for a walk with Cesare.' Fiona smiled weakly at her friend. 'I'm going to settle Ava then phone Joe. He's waiting for me phoning him when Ava's asleep.'

The Burning Question

Jinni looked surprised when Elisa told her she would be out for a short while. Reassured that Elisa had her mobile, she agreed she would leave on time when Luigi was ready to do the overnight cover, and not wait for her coming back.

Elisa and William walked along the harbour side. The air was cool and calm, and she threw a light shawl around her shoulders.

On the water hundreds of little lights twinkled from the boats moored overnight in the shelter of the harbour, and the sound of their bells tinkling sounded soothing to Elisa.

'This is such a beautiful place. I can't imagine why anyone would choose to leave,' William said.

'I guess, but the world is a big place and sometimes a small village can be suffocating,' Elisa answered remembering her own rush to leave to explore the world.

'So I take it you don't intend to stay then?' he asked.

'I didn't say that. I haven't made any further plans beyond the end of the season. Who knows, I may stay and follow in my grandfather's footsteps or I may choose to return to England.'

'To the rain and the cold? Are you mad?' William asked.

'Ah, but we can get rain and cold here, too, and further up in the hills and mountains snow like you wouldn't believe.' Elisa smiled. 'What about you, what brings you to this part of the world?'

'The house market, pure and simple, I'm afraid. I worked in the south but the market in the north suits me better,' William answered.

'I suppose that doesn't surprise me. It's a very popular area with holidaymakers both summer and winter,' Elisa said.

They reached a quiet bar and William suggested a nightcap.

'No, thanks, no alcohol, but I'll have a coffee,' Elisa offered.

'Did your grandfather have any further plans for the hotel?' William asked as they drank their coffees.

Elisa laughed.

'My grandfather always had plans, he just had that personality. He was a contented person, but he knew nothing stayed the same especially in business and he planned ahead. It was a formula that worked for him. He was incredibly astute and positive in his plans.'

'I'm sorry I never got to meet him,' William said, looking at Elisa. 'He sounds quite a character. What was his next step with the hotel, do you think?'

Elisa looked out across the lake before she spoke. She found it difficult discussing her grandfather with someone who didn't know him. She couldn't convey the essence of the man she had loved so dearly, and it made her feel uncomfortable.

'Well, there's a piece of land that runs alongside the hotel, and he considered purchasing it just in case he wanted to extend, that was just him, and I suppose it kept him young planning for the future,' she answered, hoping William would stop talking about Stephano, but she was too polite to ask him to change the subject.

'Hmm, that's interesting, maybe it's something I could help with? If you intend staying, that is,' William suggested.

'Thank you, but for the moment I think I have enough on my plate. Speaking of which it's time I headed back to the hotel. It's an early start for me in the morning.' Elisa stood ready to leave.

'I'll walk you back,' William offered.

'No, I'm fine walking on my own,' Elisa said.

'I insist.' William held out his arm for her to take.

Arm in arm they strolled back to the hotel. To her relief he chatted about everyday things and Elisa enjoyed his easy charm, and gentle humour.

'Thank you, William, walking has cleared my head,' Elisa said.

'Good, can I see you tomorrow then?' he asked moving closer until his lips were almost on hers.

'No.' She jumped back. 'I'm sorry, William. I'm not ready for a relationship.'

'No problem, Elisa, I'll be around for a long time and I have patience.' William kissed the back of her hand and turned still smiling towards her as he left the hotel.

Elisa was shaken and felt foolish at the same time. William had attempted to kiss her and she panicked spluttering about a relationship — for goodness' sake, it was only a kiss, not a proposal. What an idiot he must think she was.

★   ★   ★

As Elisa approached the kitchen she could hear the staff talking. Something in their tone made her stop to listen before going in.

She could hear Roberto talking to his sister Jinni.

'Do you think Elisa will keep the hotel open? I know she has assured us the hotel is still bringing in money but is she up to running it, and where will she do it from — here or England?

'It is all very worrying, Jinni. I have a family to think of, as do you. I loved Stephano with all my heart, and I want to be loyal to Elisa, too. I hope she decides to stay. Do you think she will?'

'I'm not sure, Roberto, at first I thought yes, then no, then when Cesare showed interest in her it was yes again. I have never known Cesare to look so love-struck.

'I don't know who this William is, or why Elisa was out with him. It was out of character for her. I'm not sure I like him, although he is based here so if she likes him it might make her stay.

'Looking at Michael and that woman Lauren, Elisa's judgement in men isn't too good,' she continued. 'Did you know he was her ex-boyfriend, and Lauren is his new girlfriend? Lauren told me all about it when I was covering reception.

'I told her I did not wish to know but she is difficult to stop talking. She seemed desperate to gossip about Elisa. I don't trust her, either. Poor Elisa, she has had such a difficult time. I wish we could help her, she has a sadness about her, and as I said poor judgement in men,' Jinni chattered back to her brother.

'Unlike yours.' Roberto laughed. 'Married to your childhood sweetheart.'

Jinni laughed, too.

'Yes, look at me, three boisterous boys, a husband who works long shifts on the road driving holiday coaches. Thank heavens for my mother-in-law looking after them.

'Well, we know we've got until the end of the season. I hope Elisa will have made up her mind by then. I hope she finds peace in her heart to let her make the correct decision for her.'

'Don't fret,' Roberto consoled her. 'She is Stephano's granddaughter. I'm sure she will have inherited his sense — she just needs to let Asolto work her magic, you'll see.'

'When did you get so sensible?' Jinni asked. 'Come on, walk me home and tell me all about my niece and nephew and their adventures.'

Elisa moved towards the reception area. Luigi was on duty.

'Good evening,' he said as Elisa approached.

'Good evening, Luigi,' Elisa replied automatically, her thoughts still on the overheard conversation.

'Jinni left a message for you. She said Cesare came back into the hotel to speak to you.'

'Thanks, Luigi.' As she moved away the message hit her. 'Luigi, do you know what Cesare wanted?'

'No, Elisa, sorry. She told him you were out with the gentleman.'

Elisa said goodnight and made her

way to her apartment as Stella came into the reception with Luigi's flask and snack for his overnight shift.

'Goodnight, Elisa. Don't look so worried. Things will work out, you'll see. They always do.'

Elisa smiled and hugged the older woman, taking comfort from her words as she made her way to bed. Her head was a whirl of thoughts. So much had happened this evening she found herself struggling to think clearly.

In reception Luigi asked Stella if Elisa gave any indication of her plans for the hotel.

'We can't hurry her decision, it will take time,' Stella answered. 'She has too much to deal with just now. She is still grieving, but I have faith she is a sensible girl.

'The best we can do is keep the hotel functioning as normal to ensure standards don't slip and let her see she has a good workforce here, that may be enough to sway her to keep it going. If only we could buy it ourselves.'

Luigi sighed.

'Maybe that would have been an idea years ago, but I am looking forward to retirement, not taking on more work, and you are busy with our grandchildren. Stephano built this hotel himself but it came at a price, we have our family and for that I am very grateful.'

Stella hugged him in agreement.

'What will we do? Should we look for other jobs just now? I like the hotel — it's just like working with family. In fact, some of them are family. What if we get a new boss or a big chain of hotels take over and we have to wear strange uniforms and all be miserable at work?'

'Are you sure we shouldn't ask her just now?' Luigi asked. 'Then we could make plans. I miss Stephano. We should have realised he was getting tired and that he couldn't go on for ever but he was so vibrant and loved this hotel and the guests that I suppose we felt he would go on forever and the hotel, too, nothing would change. We were a bit selfish thinking it could all go on for ever.'

'We were selfish and he was stubborn,' his wife said. 'We just need to give her a bit more time. She's one of us, Luigi, whether she realises it or not. Hotel Perlino is her home. The question is, does she want to stay here?'

Fear of Rejection

Lauren looked at her mobile phone as it beeped with a text message.

'Call me.'

Michael was snoring after too much wine. She moved into the bathroom to call, and listened as the number rang out. She expected the sender of the text would be angry but it didn't matter to her. She was in charge of her actions and would answer to no-one.

'What on earth were you thinking pulling a stunt like that with the child?' William's voice hissed down the line as he answered the call.

'Wasn't that hilarious? It wasn't planned, the opportunity just arose. You know I wouldn't have caused any harm to the child. But did you see the fear in Elisa's eyes?' Lauren laughed. 'Anyway, you're one to talk, I saw you trying to steal a kiss.

'Just watch you don't move too fast and put her off,' she continued, 'and don't even think about falling for her.

'And watch out for that inspector guy. I think he's got a soft spot for her, and that could be problematic. He worries me but I refuse to let him intimidate me. Michael says I've to keep away from them. He's annoyed I booked this hotel, even though I have sworn it's coincidence and how would I have known Elisa would be here. I might just have convinced him,' Lauren whispered into the phone, concerned her voice could waken Michael.

'I still don't understand why you felt it necessary to come over here. I've everything under control and now thanks to you, we need to move fast before someone puts two and two together.

'On the brighter side, after my conversation with Elisa tonight, I think another little opportunity has just arisen. I'll be in touch but please try to keep out of trouble. You don't want the inspector or dopey Michael becoming suspicious,' William cautioned her as he ended the call.

Lauren stared at the blank screen of her mobile phone. Who was William to dictate to her to keep out of trouble? She had every intention of causing trouble for Elisa and the sooner the better. She didn't have time to wait for William to romance her.

★　★　★

Cesare spent the night tossing and turning. He regretted being so harsh on Elisa without listening to her explanation. The sight of her laughing with that man had thrown him. Instead of being pleased to see her relaxed and enjoying herself, he had reacted like a sullen child.

It was all his own fault, of course. Without speaking to her, he decided she wasn't ready to move on from all that had happened to her. The pain of jealousy shocked him that she seemed so carefree with this stranger.

The force of it made him admit to himself his feelings towards her, that he wanted to be more than just a friend to her. Too late he realised how badly he had behaved, and returned to apologise, only to find she had left with William.

He shook his head in anguish as he realised he was comparing her to his ex-girfriend, a nurse, whom he had a serious relationship with whilst living in Rome. Cesare winced at the memory of her betrayal.

Two years into their relationship Cesare proposed marriage and dared to plan their future together. It came as a dreadful blow to discover she didn't share his excitement or dreams.

His stomach lurched at the memory of her confession of her relationship with a colleague, a doctor, and his heartbreak as she handed him back his ring. He thought his heart had broken, the physical pain was so severe.

He stumbled through the time that

followed until unexpectedly the prospect to take up the post of inspector in Asolto arose, and Cesare jumped at the opportunity, and so he came home to lick his wounds and recover.

Although he occasionally dated, he avoided becoming romantically involved with anyone, and his occasional brusqueness was an expression of the protective wall around his heart. The Hotel Perlino helped in his recovery and he valued his time with Stephano. His wisdom and experience of life proved invaluable.

Cesare learned how the deep pain that Stephano and Rosa faced at losing their child made them stronger as a couple, and the joy Elisa brought to their lives was palpable.

Stephano shared his concerns about Elisa being left alone in the world when he was no longer here. He asked Cesare to try to look out for her even if it was from a distance, he needed the reassurance she would have someone who cared for her.

Stephano recognised in Elisa a work ethic that drove her to build her own strong foundation in her career and life as she experienced first hand the shifting sands of life.

So it pleased him that she had a partner and he looked forward to meeting Michael. He wanted to reassure himself she had found someone who would treasure her as much as he did, and looked forward to speaking with him. Cesare felt grateful that Stephano was spared the upset of their break up.

Cesare knew that family love and support helped him through the heartache in his life, and he hoped her return to Hotel Perlino would also help Elisa heal.

The pace of life and feeling of community in Asolto was unique, and if you allowed the love in, sooner or later the pain passed. Unless of course she wanted to leave, and return to her career in England, then maybe she would put the hotel up for sale.

Cesare felt that would be a loss to her and the staff at the hotel, but he could see how the relationship with Fiona and Ava was important to Elisa. They were as close as family to her and she needed them in her life.

It surprised Cesare to discover there was an uncle that Stephano had kept hidden from Elisa. He wondered just how much Stephano knew about the uncle and his reasons for keeping Elisa protected from him. Stephano was not a vindictive man and he knew only too well the importance of family so he must have made a difficult decision in denying Elisa the opportunity of meeting her mother's brother. It was also strange the uncle had never come looking for Elisa — she was his sister's child, after all. Surely he realised the devastation the accident had caused in Elisa's life.

Cesare reasoned from the reports sent to him that the uncle was a bad lot. Theft and fraud and alcohol seemed to be his downfall. Perceptive as ever,

Stephano shielded Elisa from further harm in her childhood, but Cesare knew that deception would have been painful to his old friend.

But now Elisa was a woman, not a child, and she needed to be made aware of this other piece of information Cesare had uncovered. She needed to make her own decisions, but Cesare also needed to be sure he had all the facts to hand to help her do that, if only he could figure it out himself, before presenting it to her.

At the moment he couldn't quite tie it all together, the detective in him wanted to have the evidence and not speculation.

He must try to see Elisa first thing in the morning and try to put things right between them. He valued their friendship. Even as young adults he had been drawn to her vitality and was saddened when she left for England, taking with her his teenage heart. The teenager was now a man and a man who respected his old friend Stephano too much not to try to be a friend to his granddaughter. He would speak with her tomorrow, apologise for his bad behaviour, and try to rebuild their friendship.

Cesare gave up on his attempt to sleep and rising from his bed he looked at notes from one of his officers, who was assisting in a case.

He smiled, pleased that all was going well, and he would soon have the evidence he needed to conclude this part. He was proud of his team, he was happy in his job, they were tenacious together and showed no fear.

So what was the brave detective frightened of now in meeting with Elisa? Why did her opinion of him matter so much to him? The answer was plain to him — he feared her rejection. He feared she would reject his friendship, and his promise to Stephano would be broken.

He gripped the edge of his desk, acknowledging to himself the painful truth. He didn't fear the loss of her friendship. Slowly he turned and faced himself in the mirror. Be honest, Cesare, you don't want friendship, you're in love with her, that is the rejection you fear, so what are you going to do about it? Hide to avoid the heartbreak? No, Cesare, you are going to fight for her, that's what you're going to do. You're not going to lose her again.

But first things first. He must see Elisa and tell her of his discovery . . . that Lauren was her cousin.

No Love Lost

Confused by her feeling towards William and by Cesare's behaviour, Elisa spent a disturbed night. As she tossed and turned and sleep evaded her, an idea played around the edges of her mind.

Little snippets dipped in and out of her consciousness . . . Would this work? Could that happen? The hotel . . . it was all about the hotel, but which hotel, what country did she see herself in when she imagined her plans taking shape? There was a man helping her but who was he? She couldn't see his face.

When her alarm sounded, she rose exhausted but certain she must meet with Cesare to explain what had occurred the previous evening. She understood his anger. It was unforgivable of her to forget to invite him after all he had done for her. She just expected him to be there without needing an invitation. To make it worse he appeared in time to witness her enjoying William's company. Well, there was no crime in that, she told herself.

She also needed to understand what happened when she froze when William tried to kiss her. Was she attracted to William? He was good-looking, no doubt about it. He was also very charming, maybe too charming, or was he just familiar and reminded her of England? Maybe she just needed to be with someone who didn't feel sorry for her. Whatever the reason it indicated she wasn't ready to take things further.

She never was a girl who participated in casual relationships, but he indicated he would be around for a long time. But what exactly did that mean? Did he intend to move to Italy on a permanent basis? For work, for love?

Elisa laughed to herself. Now you are getting carried away, she told herself. William's easy charm didn't sit well with her. Oh, she enjoyed it, was flattered by it but it felt superficial to her. It made her suspicious that he could fall so easily into forming a relationship with her, where he felt comfortable enough to kiss her.

Elisa wasn't like that. She took time to get to know people and once she did she was a loyal friend to them unless they hurt her and then she could cut them off completely — as she was trying to do with Michael if only Lauren would let her.

Time was running out for her to decide her future, and the future of Hotel Perlino. The decision lay heavy on her as she knew she held the livelihood of the staff in her hands. She needed to speak to someone she could trust who didn't have an interest in the hotel.

Perhaps that was the reason she had been a little out of character last night, in agreeing to go for a walk with William. She just wanted to kick her heels back a little bit with someone who didn't know anything about the hotel or her grandfather. Now she felt guilty for feeling that way, and she certainly didn't feel William was someone she had built up a trust with.

As she remembered last night she thought of Cesare. The hurt in his brown eyes was evident and she regretted causing it. She cared for him and would never have deliberately hurt him for the world.

She recalled the way he handled the situation when Ava was missing. His patience and gentleness with Ava when she was found was so like her grandfather. A memory of Signora Ricci complimenting Cesare came to her.

'He's a good man. We are lucky to have him looking after us. Your grandfather was very fond of him, as was your grandmother. She was my friend and I miss her friendship. Why don't you come visit with me next week for lunch, take yourself away from here? I can tell you tales of your grandparents and you can admire my photos of all my grandchildren — all ten of them.'

Elisa had laughed with her at her last comment. She should visit with her, it would be comforting to speak with her about her grandparents. She had only a vague recollection of the Riccis being friends with her grandparents. Like most children in the village they spent little time listening to adult conversations, there were so many other more exciting things to do or explore outdoors.

Despite the events of the previous night Elisa still had a hotel to run, and she forced herself to stop thinking of herself and get to work dealing with hotel business.

She shared a quick breakfast with Fiona and Ava, who showed no sign of being affected by her adventure the previous evening. Fiona, like Elisa, had experienced a disturbed night.

'I hope this hasn't put you off the hotel,' Elisa said as they drank coffee.

'No, of course not. It was just a bit unsettling. But today is a new day the sun is shining and we are going swimming, aren't we, missy.' Fiona tickled Ava as she spoke.

'Yes, in the pool with my water wings.' Ava squealed with delight.

'That sounds like a great idea. I wish I could join in but I have so much to do. You girls have fun without me,' Elisa said as she kissed the top of Ava's head and hugged her friend.

Elisa was in the office when she had a call from reception that someone wanted to speak to her. Assuming it was a guest with an issue reception couldn't deal with, Elisa immediately rushed through prepared to resolve whatever the incident was. There was no incident. Michael was waiting for her and he was alone.

'How can I help you?' Elisa refrained from calling him sir, not out of rudeness but it felt silly given the circumstances and would have come over as petty.

'Can we have a chat, Elisa?' He was uncomfortable and aware of staff listening in to the conversation.

'Of course,' Elisa said. 'Is something wrong with your room?'

'It's not about our room or the hotel. I would like to chat if that's possible.'

'OK, well, shall we sit over at a table, then?'

'Thank you.' Michael followed as Elisa led the way to a table in the corner. She didn't order any refreshments for them. She had no intention of staying longer than was necessary. She wondered where Lauren was hiding.

'Lauren has gone shopping,' Michael said, sensing her curiosity.

'What would you like to talk about, Michael? As you can see, I have a hotel to run and I am very busy.'

'Yes, I can see. It's a beautiful hotel and you're doing a marvellous job. I'm very proud of you.'

'I beg your pardon, Michael, but I don't need your approval. Now please get on with it.' Elisa didn't wish to be close to Michael for any longer than was necessary. If he had chosen to take the opportunity to speak with her whilst Lauren was elsewhere then she was not interested. If he wanted to talk about all that happened between them then she was beginning to lose patience with him.

'About last night . . . I'm sorry. I don't know why Lauren did that with Ava. I'm sure it wasn't intentional and that she didn't mean to frighten everyone but all the same it was wrong and I'm sorry.'

'You don't have anything to apologise for in relation to Ava's disappearance. You didn't do anything other than bring that woman into Ava's life. It's she who should be apologising for the alarm she caused. As for everything else, well, let's just move on.'

'No, Elisa. I mean yes, let's move on if that's what you want. But I do need to explain. I'm sorry for what happened. I'm not sure how it happened but it did and that's my responsibility and something I need to live with. But also for coming here.

'I didn't realise this was your family hotel. I had time off work and Lauren suggested we take a quick break. We both needed one. I didn't pay attention when she announced it was all booked. I think I've been in shock these past few weeks, everything has moved so fast.'

Elisa refrained from screaming at him that he wasn't the only one to have experienced shock in the last few weeks. Instead she remained calm.

'It's all in the past, Michael,' she said. 'Once we've sold the flat then that's our connection over. Hopefully it will sell soon and you and Lauren can find a place together.'

Michael made a noise.

'I'm not sure we're totally suited. I shouldn't have done that to you. I'm so sorry, Elisa.'

'Well this is a conversation you need to have with her, Michael, not me. Now I need to get back to work. Good luck.' Elisa stood up and moved towards the office behind the reception. She stopped as she reached the doorway and turned back. Michael was where she left him, sitting staring on to the polished tiles.

The part of her that loved him once felt sorry for him. Then she remembered he had brought it on himself and had caused her considerable pain along the way. Her sympathy disappeared fast.

Box of Treasures

The ringing of her mobile telephone disturbed Elisa's thoughts.

'Good morning,' William said when she answered.

'Hi,' she answered back, 'how are you?'

'I'm good and I have fantastic news. Michael has agreed on the valuation of the flat so we can move on getting the paperwork signed, if you want to go ahead with it?'

'Oh.' The sound left Elisa's throat before she could prevent it. She found it strange Michael had been sitting in front of her yet hadn't thought to mention he had spoken with William about the flat.

'You don't sound sure about it,' William said.

'It's just so final, something else in my life ending.' Elisa sat down as she spoke. Despite her conversation with Michael it was still a shock that it was actually happening.

'I'm sorry, Elisa. Look, why don't I take care of getting the papers drawn up? I'll arrange for Michael to sign them, and then meet with you for you to sign. Would that be better, then you wouldn't need to have any awkward conversations with him? He transfers the money to your account and you're free of him,' William suggested.

'I'll have to check with Signor Ricci.' Elisa wavered.

'I'll speak to him, tell him how distressing this all is for you, and ask if he'll allow me to help you with it. Do you want to come to the office today? We can speak to Mr Ricci next door together if that would reassure you.' William's voice was softer now as he spoke.

'I'm too busy today,' Elisa said, her voice taut. She wanted this call to finish. She wasn't ready to do this.

'OK, I'll do what I can with the

paperwork today. Oh, another thing I almost forgot to tell you. My colleague has told me he knows who owns the land next to the hotel, and that the owner is very keen to sell.

'I've made an appointment with him today, just to get a heads up on it, to be ready for when it goes on the market so you'll get first chance to make an offer if it's something you would be interested in.

'Must dash now, I'm showing a house to another British couple desperate to live the Italian dream.' He laughed. 'Speak to you soon or even better see you tonight. Ciao, babe.'

He had rung off before she could reply.

'Ciao, babe,' she muttered. That phrase jarred with her when it was used so casually often by people who couldn't be bothered remembering the names of the people they were speaking to and for some reason she found his tone disrespectful.

Irritated and exhausted by lack of

sleep, William's flow of information had frazzled her brain. It was all moving too fast for her, and she couldn't think straight. She couldn't take it all in. She was feeling rushed and she didn't like that feeling. Elisa liked to be in control.

The overheard conversation between Jinni and Roberto was also playing on Elisa's mind and she decided she needed to find out more about the staff's hopes and fears for the future of the hotel. She knew it was unfair they should suffer due to her lack of decision making on her future, and that last thing she needed at the height of the season was stressed staff, or worse, losing staff to a rival hotel.

She had a responsibility for their welfare, something Stephano took very seriously, not to mention a debt of loyalty to them. Despite her exhaustion she decided the best thing to do would be to hold an informal meeting in the dining-room at a quieter part of the day and when the majority of the guests had gone on a day trip.

The incident with Ava demonstrated to Elisa how the staff worked as a team with little effort. They just slotted into place, listened for instructions and followed them. She needed to thank them for that too.

In fact, Elisa realised she needed to thank them for a whole lot more. Their efforts kept the hotel running smoothly in those early weeks following her grandfather's death and probably for some time before.

So lost in her own grief and change of circumstances she hadn't really acknowledged their loss too. She would put that right at their meeting. She would speak to Stella and Jinni to book an appropriate time in the diary.

Elisa decided she had another task to face — the painful one of going through her grandfather's private papers, which were locked away in his big writing desk in the office.

Maybe he would have notes on what he spoke to staff about and how much he shared with them.

Stella had given her the key to his desk on her arrival at the hotel following Stephano's death. She had already seen the accountant's reports and had a good idea of the overview of the business accounts, she also checked the cash flow on a daily basis. She knew from a financial point of view the business was healthy. From experience she also knew nothing stayed the same, particularly in the world of tourism and travel.

Elisa braced herself to study the old ledgers and notebooks. She needed to find the spirit of her nonno in them and perhaps to discover his thoughts and plans for the future of the hotel.

Why, she asked herself again and again, didn't she have this conversation with him when she had the opportunity?

Taking a break from the current day-to-day business, she poured herself a coffee and, seated in her grandfather's favourite chair, she began working her way through the books.

The familiar writing momentarily took her breath away and she gripped the edge of the desk until she felt able to continue.

In a huge envelope she discovered old faded papers yellow around the edges, and her breath caught in her throat to discover they were the original plans for the hotel and she could see where her grandparents' hopes and dreams had begun and where they had grown as the business grew and they could afford to expand.

Her heart skipped a beat as she came across an envelope marked 'My children's homes'.

With shaking hands she withdrew the contents and there were the plans for her parents' and her uncle and aunt's homes. The sadness overwhelmed her as she thought of Stephano planning for his children's future, ensuring they had a roof over their heads, something he had worked long and hard to provide for his family and then to have those plans cruelly snatched from him by a car accident.

Elisa studied the plans and noticed the parcel of land Stephano had identified for building was the same one he later spoke about building an extension on.

She rummaged amongst the books and papers and found the extension plans. She placed both sets of plans to one side, deciding she would study them in more detail later.

As she read through Stephano's notes she found indications that he, too, realised that the market could change at any time.

She found various minutes from meetings held in relation to keeping the hotel open during the winter to cover the skiing season amongst other ideas.

It made her smile to picture Stephano poring over future plans, and proud, also that he was forward thinking — not for him the easy life of sitting back and taking it easy, it wasn't his way.

Elisa had been poring over books for

a few hours, taking her own notes, when she came across a box file that seemed out of place.

Lifting it from its hiding place in the depths of the drawer she gasped as she read her own name written in her nonno's writing on the front. With shaking fingers she opened the file.

She could not believe her eyes as reminders of her life tumbled on to the desk. She could hear her heart beat as though from a far way off and for a moment she thought she might pass out.

Clutching the desk to steady herself she wept when she saw the keepsakes her grandfather had carefully stored. Drawings from her nursery days. Birthday and Christmas cards in her childish writing. Little notes passed between them, her school reports, and her letters from university.

Her life was contained in this little box that her nonno had kept near him. She sobbed to think of him keeping it safe and wondered did he look at it and remember her, did he miss her when he remembered happier times when he had his Rosa and Elisa with him.

Once more she regretted the wasted time when she should have been with him, creating more memories and talking together. Oh, how much she yearned to talk to him just one more time.

As she was sifting through the contents an envelope fell on to her lap. Elisa could see it was new, not old and faded like the other contents. As she turned it over her heart skipped a beat as she saw her name written on the front in Stephano's handwriting.

With shaking fingers she opened the envelope.

Listen to Your Heart

'Vita mia,' Elisa read. She felt a lump rise in her throat at her grandfather calling her his life.

'My darling girl,' the letter continued, 'if you are reading this then it means I am no longer with you. Do not be sad for me. I have gone to join my beloved Rosa, she is waiting for me, and I am ready to meet her again. My only sorrow is to leave you alone in this world.'

Tears dropped on the paper and Elisa didn't try to stop them.

'It is my dearest wish that you follow your own path in this world. Do not be tied to Hotel Perlino. If you wish to be part of it, that is all well and good. If not, then do not have regrets or worries. This was my life, it does not have to be yours.

'I only ask that you treat my loyal

staff fairly. They have served this family well and deserve respect for all they have done. Stella and Luigi are family in all but name. I know you will do the right thing by them.

'Take counsel from my good friend Antonio Ricci. He is a wise man, and his wife Maria will be as good a friend to you as she was to my Rosa, I have no doubt.

'Also my very good friend Cesare has promised me he will look out for you and help if you need him. He is a good man, Elisa. I remember the two of you playing together as children.

'Rosa and I called him your shadow, always patiently waiting for you to make the first move then he would follow you into whatever adventures you had chosen for the day.'

Elisa was touched that her nonno remembered her childhood antics and recalled herself the presence of Cesare in her younger days. Never far from her side, he had his own ideas but was happy to let her take the lead and able to rein her in if she strayed too close to danger.

'I was sorry when you left for university but proud that you stood on your own feet away from Asolto. It would have been an easy path for you to follow here, but you have proved yourself able to work from the bottom up and I respect you for that and others do too. I was alone without you, but I was never lonely, Elisa, you brightened my life with your calls and letters. You brought me so much joy.

'Your mother was a good and beautiful woman and I see her in you. I also see my son Alessandro. You have his determination and single-mindedness. Alessandro had big plans for this hotel. He wanted to move into winter opening and expand.'

Elisa looked at the notebooks in Stephano's writing and realised he was following her father's plans for the hotel. It pleased her to think of them both collaborating on the hotel's future, and for Stephano to keep her father's dream alive in his plans.

'And now to you, my little mouse. You will have worked out by now that I didn't disclose the existence of your mother's brother, your uncle.

'I have no wish to discredit him but suffice to say he would have brought no joy to your life, and I ask that you trust me on the decision I made on your behalf to cut him out of your life. If I did wrong, please forgive me, my child.

'When it fell to us to care for you it was as though we had been given a second chance. The honour of raising our son's child was so precious a gift to Rosa and I, that we were initially overwhelmed. But you were such a sweet child and you brought so much joy into our lives we couldn't bear to think someone could take that away from us or bring another moment of sadness into your life.'

Elisa stopped reading to catch her breath. To think her grandfather still worried over his decision about her uncle, saddened her. She trusted him with all her heart and could only believe he made his decision with the best of intentions.

Stephano was never a vindictive man, he made decisions taking all sides into account and he took his time. It must have caused him great sorrow to cut her off from her mother's only relative but she knew he had his reasons. He protected her.

'Elisa, I hope that like Rosa and I, you find that one true love that will last you a lifetime. That's what carries us through this life, love. Oh, it hurts, but there is nothing to be gained by living life without some pain.

'Only then can we truly treasure the good times. Only then can we appreciate other people, and help them on their way out of the bad times and they us. Choose carefully, my little mouse, but never be afraid. You will know when you have found the right one for you, everything will click into place.

'You are free, my child. Free to move on away from Italy. Free to stay if you choose. Whatever your decision know that my love will always be with you.

'Nonno.

'Xx'

The dam broke and Elisa sobbed so hard it hurt her throat. Great racking sobs that left her breathless and exhausted. This precious gift of a letter from her grandfather, full of love and hope, had brought together everything she was struggling with.

There was a gentle knock on the door and Stella's face appeared concerned.

'Are you OK, my little potato? I thought I heard crying. Oh, my Elisa, are you all right?' Stella crossed the room and grasped Elisa pulling her into her arms. 'Let it all out, it's OK, little one.' Stella held Elisa until she stopped sobbing and was able to breathe again.

'Thank you, Stella. I was just overcome at Nonno's words.' Elisa dabbed at her eyes with a tissue.

'I understand it has all just caught up with you. You will feel better now,' Stella answered. 'It is only natural. I am going to get you a cool drink, and then I insist you lie down for an hour or so, you are worn out. We can manage here while you rest.'

'Thank you, Stella. I am tired. A lie down will help me.' Elisa smiled weakly.

As Stella left to get her a drink. Elisa collected the papers and stored them back in their boxes.

'Thank you, Nonno,' she whispered as she gently kissed his words to her as she placed his letter to her with them.

She locked his desk and collecting her drink from Stella who gave her a supportive smile she made her way to her apartment, grateful Fiona and Ava were out.

Despite her head swimming with her discovery of her grandfather's plans and his letter to her, she fell into a sound sleep.

★ ★ ★

The sound of Ava crying in the next room woke her. Elisa was surprised to discover she had been asleep for two hours. Jumping up from bed she made her way into the lounge area of the apartment feeling refreshed from her long nap.

'Hey, what's wrong with my favourite girl?' Elisa asked.

'Mummy says Daddy is coming here today,' Ava answered through sobs.

'Yes, he is. Don't you want to see Daddy? I'm sure he wants to see you,' Elisa said, lifting Ava into her arms.

'Yes, I do. But Mummy says that then we will all go home together,' Ava said.

'Don't you want to go home?' Elisa asked.

'No, I want to stay here.'

'But what about all your friends? Wouldn't you miss them?'

'Yes, but you won't be there.'

'Won't I?'

'No. Mummy told Daddy she thinks that you're going to stay here.'

Fiona blushed.

'I can't deny it — she caught me.'

'Oh, Ava sweetheart, Auntie Elisa

needs to decide where she wants to live. You know how it feels when you can only take one toy with you when you go to visit your friends? Well, it's a bit like that. I want to stay in both places but I can't, and whichever choice I make, it doesn't mean that I love the other one any less. Do you understand?'

'No,' Ava answered.

Elisa laughed.

'Neither do I. Why don't we wait until I have decided and then I'll try to explain it to you? But tell me something, Ava, do you like living here?'

'Yes, it's the best. I wish I could stay here for ever.' Ava jumped up and down.

Fiona looked surprised.

'Ava, do you mean that?'

'Yes, Mummy. I think you and Daddy should just buy a house here like Auntie Elisa. Then Auntie Elisa could marry Cesare and we could all stay together.' Ava hugged Fiona.

'Ava,' Fiona said, 'that's enough.'

Elisa bent over and kissed Ava on top of her little blonde head.

'Oh, Ava, if only life was that simple,' Elisa said.

Ava's words stayed with Elisa causing her to be distracted, and Fiona asked twice if she was OK.

'I'm just tired,' she said giving her a weak smile. 'I had a bit of a melt-down today.' She explained to Fiona about Stephano's boxes.

'Oh, Elisa, I wish I had been here to help you.' Fiona hugged her friend.

'You're here now, Fiona, and having you and Ava close is a comfort,' Elisa said. 'But right now I better check what's been happening whilst I snoozed.' Elisa laughed.

★ ★ ★

In reception Stella greeted her with a hug and assured her all was well.

'Thank you, Stella, for looking after me.' Elisa held the older woman in an embrace.

'It's OK, you are like one of my own children, which is why I can tell it's an added strain having Michael and that woman staying in the hotel, isn't it?' Stella said. 'I don't know how you manage. She doesn't even try to keep a low profile. She gives the staff in the restaurant and bar a difficult time, always complaining. Thankfully the other guests more than make up for her bad manners with their compliments.'

'It won't be for long and we will make sure we don't take a booking from them again,' Elisa answered.

'Shall we be taking bookings for next season, Elisa?' Stella asked. 'I know you have had a lot to deal with but rumours are flying that we are being taken over. I try to reassure staff but you know how people talk.'

'Oh, Stella, I don't know what I'm doing yet. That's bad of me, I know, but there's so much to weigh up. I have a good career back home.'

'Back home . . . maybe that's an indication of how you are thinking, my little potato. This is home to us. Is England home to you? Can you manage a career in England and a hotel in Italy?' Stella reached out and held Elisa in her arms.

'Listen to your heart, but act with your head. It's what your nonno would have done.'

Elisa lifted the photograph of her grandfather, which was kept at reception. She ran her fingers over the glass and again wished she could stroke the face she so loved, just as she had done as a child.

Stephano smiled back at her, proud and smart in his shirt and tie, a man who had faced the challenges that life had thrown at him.

When times were hard he found a way to keep moving around the problem, and then forward until the time came when he was strong enough to move up and over the problem. He listened to the advice of those he trusted, and made his decisions based on good information.

Elisa wavered for a few moments then on an impulse, she phoned Signora Ricci and asked if today would be a good day to call on her.

A Friend in Need

William moved fast. His first appointment that morning was showing a hillside house to a British couple who were keen to buy in the area. The owner was a younger man who inherited the house from his father.

He worked in Milan and had bought a more fashionable home for his family. He considered keeping it as a family home, but decided that the market was right to sell.

All going to plan — William rubbed his hands together — he could close this deal. With the sale of Elisa's flat and the purchase of the land for her by the end of the week, it could prove a profitable few days.

Since he began working in the area at the start of the season, he found it rather mundane. However, it gave him the opportunity to put in place his future plans.

As he drove through the countryside he considered Lauren. She should have stayed in England and not brought her love interest to Italy.

It caused him additional work, especially the incident with the little girl drawing attention to them and involving the inspector. It wasn't helpful, and the inspector, Cesare, he was a strange one. Dark and foreboding, it was clear he harboured feelings for Elisa. William couldn't fathom Elisa's feelings for the inspector but his hesitancy in making a move was William's good fortune.

In William's opinion Elisa just needed a little time, a bit of tender loving care, a bit of sweet-talking and the world would be William's oyster.

As he arrived at the hill top house the owner was there to greet him. The couple arrived soon after and fell in love with the property at once. So overtaken were they with the beauty of the area that with a little bit of persuasion from William they made an offer on the spot, subject to all the paperwork being completed.

William confidently answered all their questions about the transfer of funds and timescales. Both parties were keen to settle quickly, and William reassured them he could arrange a quick transaction agreeable to both parties. Bingo, William thought — one down, two to go.

★ ★ ★

Signora Ricci welcomed Elisa into her home, which as she described was filled with photos of her family.

'Forgive me,' she said, 'I am a proud grandmother just as Rosa was.'

'Do you see them often, Signora Ricci?' Elisa asked, smiling at all the differing ages of the children from thirty-somethings down to babies.

'Please, you must call me Maria. Not so much of them during the week, but they all come on Sunday and the house and garden are left in chaos, and Antonio, Signor Ricci, says he can't think with the noise, but he loves it really.'

'I feel bad that my grandparents didn't have that,' Elisa said. 'They loved children so much.'

'They may not have had you running about causing trouble on a Sunday, but they had your love and they loved you so very much, it shone out of them when they spoke of you.' Maria patted Elisa's hand.

'Your grandmother suffered much on the loss of her child,' Maria added, 'but she poured love into you and she was also well loved in the community as was your grandfather. They did so much to help.

'When the tourist season was over they hosted lunches and dances for older people from this town and beyond and Christmas parties for the children in the area and they raised money to buy gifts and presents for the hospitals.

'Whatever was needed, they were there, usually with Stella, Luigi and even Cesare helping, whether they wanted to or not.'

'I remember as a child and student helping them with some of their charity works, but I didn't know half of what they did. That's terrible of me, isn't it?'

'No, they had their life and you had yours. That's how it should be. We raise our children to leave the nest. They were proud you learned to soar and fly, my little one.'

'Now,' Maria took both Elisa's hands in hers and looked her straight in the eye, 'tell me what is really troubling you, my dear.'

Before she could stop, Elisa poured out all her worries to the motherly Signora Ricci. The concern over the future of the hotel, where her future should be, where to call home, Michael, William, Cesare, her uncle, she sobbed it all out.

'Do you feel better now?' Maria asked Elisa.

'Yes, thank you. I'm so sorry for doing that to you, I seem to be a bit tearful today. You must think I'm dreadful.'

'Don't ever be ashamed of tears, my dear. They show we care, and that can only be a good thing.'

Elisa hugged Maria. As the two women enjoyed the remainder of Elisa's visit over coffee and pastries, Elisa found her spirits lifted as she listened to Maria's tales of Asolto and her grandparents. Maria was an excellent storyteller with a long memory.

When Elisa had taken her leave, Signora Ricci recounted some, but not all, of her conversation with Elisa to her husband when she popped into his office to remind him not to work to late.

'I am concerned, my dear, about her making agreements with William, especially money decisions. Maybe you could persuade her to speak to you instead. I'm sure William is a lovely man, but she is vulnerable, Antonio, she is grieving and recovering from a broken romance, and vulnerable woman are easy prey to those who do not have their best interests at heart.'

Signor Ricci who had only been half listening to his wife looked up.

'I'm sure she is fine, Maria. She is a sensible girl. Just give her time to recover before you start matchmaking.'

'I know you are not listening to me, Antonio. I am not trying to encourage her into a relationship. That is her choice, although if I were her I would favour Cesare over William.'

'Maria.' Antonio tapped his pen against the papers he was reading. 'I'm a busy man,' he said although there was a hint of a smile on his lips as he spoke. He knew his wife was a hopeless romantic always trying to marry off someone, and he loved her for it.

'Yes, well, what I'm trying to say . . . ' Maria realised she had gone off subject.

'Elisa told me William has asked her to sign papers to sell her flat in England and he has spoken to the person who owns the land next to the hotel and is urging her to buy it.'

Signor Ricci looked over the top of his gold framed spectacles.

'I think you're right, dear, thank you for showing concern. She is lucky to have you as a friend. I shall indeed speak to her.'

Satisfied she had got the result she wanted, Signora Ricci left her husband's office with one final reminder for him not to be late.

After Signora Ricci left, Signor Ricci abandoned the papers before him. Deep in thought he rubbed his chin as he decided his next action. Lifting his phone he made a call.

'Cesare, I need to speak to you urgently. Can you come to my office?'

In His Kiss

Elisa returned to the hotel feeling tired but much calmer. Her visit with Signora Ricci had proved more enjoyable than she had anticipated. Her embarrassment at her outburst of crying soon disappeared with the easy-going nature of her hostess, who welcomed her into her home and into her family circle.

'You're looking a lot better,' Fiona remarked as Elisa walked on to the terrace where she and Ava were enjoying a cool drink.

'I do feel better. I don't feel quite so confused,' Elisa replied. 'But how are you? When does Joe arrive?' Elisa hugged her friend.

'Later tonight,' Fiona replied. 'Are you sure it's still OK?'

'Of course it is. Would you like me to look after Ava and let you and Joe have some time together tomorrow night?'

'That would be lovely, but Stella has already offered so you can both fight over her.' Fiona laughed.

'Oh, I'm sure I would lose that fight. Stella will have all her grandchildren fussing over her. Ava loves it here, doesn't she, Fiona?'

'Me too. What's not to like?' Fiona answered. 'I've been thinking, Elisa, if you did decide to stay, and no pressure from me, but I would like to give living here a try.'

'Do you really mean that, Fiona?' Elisa was shocked.

'Obviously I would need to talk it through with Joe but you can see how Ava is blossoming in the short time she has been here. She's more confident and she adores Stella and Luigi. Joe would love the mountain biking, too. He's always saying he never gets out enough back home.

'He could ask for a sabbatical from work. I'm sure his employers would agree given their situation, and he could pick up some surveying work here or suchlike — he's a good builder, as you know.

'We could let out our house for a year to give it a go. If we like it, great, if not then we go home. Joe never sees his family because of the distance, and mine are being forced to move away.'

'Wow!' Elisa said. 'It's a big decision to make on a whim.'

'I know but if you are here it would feel right, but as I say, no pressure.' Fiona smiled.

'We're going out to feed the ducks, Auntie Elisa,' Ava piped up, 'and then my daddy is coming to visit me tonight.'

'He'll be so excited to see you.' Elisa bent down and kissed her. 'But I'm not sure he'll recognise you.'

'Why, Auntie Elisa?'

'Well, I think you've grown so much since he last saw you, just like the sunflowers we planted last year. Do remember how tall they grew?' She indicated with her hands.

'I helped Luigi plant flowers today,' Ava said. 'He said they're mine to look after, but I'm not sure how I'm going to manage that.' Her little brow furrowed.

'Oh, Luigi will think of something, I'm sure.' Elisa laughed. 'He's very clever.'

As Elisa waved them off she made her way back to reception, intent on making a difficult phone call to Cesare. Her mind was still reeling after her conversation with Fiona, and her visit to Maria.

Before she could make the call to Cesare her mobile rang.

'Hi, Elisa,' William said when she answered.

'Oh, hi, how did the viewing go?' she asked being polite but anxious to phone Cesare.

'Great. Sealed the deal. Two happy customers and I feel like celebrating. Would you like to go for a meal or a drink tonight?'

'I'm sorry. I can't. I'm working,' Elisa answered, crossing her fingers at the lie she was telling. She knew Jinni was on duty.

'Of course. Maybe another time. Oh, and as Michael is returning home at the weekend. He is prepared to come into the office tomorrow to sign the agreement. Would you be able to come into the office too?'

'I'm not sure, William, I'm very busy, and I would like Signor Ricci to look over the paperwork before I sign,' Elisa replied.

'That's right, Elisa, I forgot, you did mention that. I'll drop them into his office, and let you know when he's approved them.

'I do have one more piece of news,' he continued. 'I met with the owner of the land next to the hotel, and he has given me some provisional figures to discuss. I'm having a survey done tomorrow. I'll have a better idea then. Why don't I meet with you tomorrow night and we can discuss the flat and the land. I could collect you at the hotel.'

'Can I call you back, William? I've got to go. I've a guest who needs my attention.' This was her second lie, and it didn't sit well with her, but she needed to end this conversation. She didn't have a customer, but she did see Cesare approaching.

Free from the irritation of William she could appreciate Cesare as he walked up the drive and into the hotel. His long powerful stride covered the distance in no time. Elisa studied his face, trying to read his attitude as he neared the reception desk. It was impossible to tell. He wore his police officer face.

'Good afternoon, signorina.'

'Good afternoon, inspector. How are you? Can I get you a cold drink?' She moved to the bar.

Cesare reached out for her, grasping her arm gently.

'I'm sorry, Elisa,' he said. 'I was harsh. There was no need for me to have treated you so badly.'

The closeness of him and the softness

of his apology was intoxicating. For the second time today Elisa felt faint.

'You did nothing wrong. I made a mistake, a moment of forgetfulness, and after all you have done for this family. It's I who should apologise. Please, Cesare, come through to the apartment.'

Unaware they were being watched, they entered the private area behind reception, and as the door closed behind them, Lauren picked up her mobile and texted William.

'We need to move fast.'

As Elisa showed Cesare into the lounge shyness came over her, catching her unawares.

'Please take a seat.' She indicated to Cesare as he moved across the room towards a chess set laid out on an occasional table. Elisa caught him looking at the chess pieces fondly and a lump came to her throat. The tears that had never been far from her throughout the day threatened to fall again.

'I miss him, Cesare, even though I

wasn't home as much as I should have been, I always felt he was just a phone call, a letter or a flight away. He was on my side, Cesare. I let him down. I should have been here,' she said.

'Stop that right now. You didn't let him down. He was so proud of you and all you had achieved. He was especially proud that you made your career on your own ability rather than staying here and just falling into a job without experiencing what you could do in the real world. 'Cesare,' he would say, 'she's finding her own value.''

'Did he really say that or are you just trying to make me feel better?'

'No, he said it. I can understand it, too. Sometimes you have to go away to come back and appreciate, and be appreciated for yourself rather than other people's expectations of what you should be or how you should act based on your childhood history. We all need to grow.'

'Is that what you did, Cesare? Go away to come home?'

'Yes, and that was Stephano's doing. He could see I would be stifled here. Oh, it would have been simple to stay, lazy even. I could have become an officer and covered the area I grew up in till it was time to retire, it would have been an easy option.

'But Stephano knew that one day I would wake up with regret that I didn't push myself to try to rise higher to work to my full ability.'

'Do you think he regretted staying here? I would hate to think that family circumstances held him back and made him stay out of a sense of duty.'

'No, Stephano was contented with his life, he told me so many times. He built a business from scratch with his beloved wife and when hard times came they worked together and raised you to be the wonderful woman you turned out to be.' Cesare smiled.

'You spent a lot of time together, didn't you?'

'Yes, we did. He was good company and a great teacher.'

'What did he teach you?'

'Oh, so many things. I had so many lessons to learn, especially when I returned home.' He laughed.

'Was it hard coming back?'

'Yes and no. No because I was ready to do the job of inspector. I had learned much away from home in often hostile situations and it moulded me into a better officer. And returning home, what better place could I choose to work? I love this area and the people in it. Asolto was always home no matter where I went.'

'And yes?' Elisa probed.

'Matters of the heart you might say. I needed a safe place to recover.' Cesare kept his head down as he spoke.

'Ah well, it seems matters of the heart brought us both home. I'm sorry you have been hurt.' Elisa reached out to touch his hand.

Her gentleness touched him, but he wasn't here for her to reassure him, it was his job to look after her.

'Home heals the heart, Elisa, believe

me. And as for Stephano always being on your side, nothing's changed, he still is, but he arranged some back up, too.' Cesare smiled a lopsided smile as he spoke. 'If you'll allow me to be on your side it would be just like old times back in school, when we watched out for each other.'

'Oh, Cesare, let's not fall out again,' Elisa said. 'I need you on my side, thank you.'

'Well that's settled then.' As Cesare smiled at her, he wanted nothing more than to hold her in his arms. To distract them both he reached and picked up a chess piece.

'He enjoyed chess, we often played during the quieter winter evenings. He taught me, told me it would keep the mind focused.' He sighed.

'He tried to teach me, too, when I was little, but my mind was too full of other nonsense,' Elisa said.

'You, full of nonsense?' Cesare turned towards her a smile twitching at the corners of his mouth. 'You had your head stuck in your books.'

'No, I didn't, not all the time,' Elisa protested.

'You sure?' Cesare persisted.

'Well, I remember one occasion I had to be rescued when I got stuck up a tree.' Elisa turned to him, her chin stuck out in defiance.

'Yeah, I remember that one too.' Cesare laughed. 'You were frightened you would get arrested for trespassing.'

Elisa blushed remembering the incident.

'I did overreact a bit, but someone calmed me and talked me through taking one step at a time and helped me down with no harm done.' She moved closer to Cesare. 'Thank you for then, and for now, Cesare.'

'Elisa,' Cesare whispered low as he brushed her hair from her face. His soft eyes looked deep into hers and he took her face in his strong hands.

Elisa lifted her face to his, her heart thumping in her chest. She wanted this man to kiss her more than anything.

Cesare brushed his lips against hers, gently then more urgently. Elisa responded. The shrill tone of her mobile disturbed the moment.

Cesare sighed as Elisa broke away from his arms to answer it.

'Oh, hi, William.'

'Hi Elisa, good news, Signor Ricci has approved the paperwork. I can bring it to you for signature now if it's suitable. Once you've agreed to the sale, you can move on with your life, Elisa.'

'Yes, yes, you're right, William, but it's not convenient just now but maybe first thing tomorrow morning. I'll call into your office. Would that be OK?'

'Sure, no problem. Now, can I change your mind about tonight, even a quick drink?' he coaxed.

'No, sorry, William. I have something I have to do after work.' She looked pointedly at Cesare as she spoke.

'OK, see you tomorrow, looking forward to it.' William smiled as he spoke but snapped his phone shut when the call was over. He needed to guarantee she signed tomorrow, and he knew because Lauren had informed him she was with the interfering police officer, he had to get this deal over the line as soon as possible.

'Why does he want you to call into his office?' Cesare asked Elisa. His body language and tone had changed from a few moments before.

Elisa recognised the professional Cesare taking over and behaving as he did on the night Ava went missing. She sensed something was wrong.

'I have papers to sign. Cesare, what is it? Is there something going on I should know about?' She faced him as she spoke, and saw the flicker of uncertainty cross his face. 'Tell me. Please.'

Cesare led her to the sofa and sat beside her. Holding her hand, he spoke.

'Elisa . . . ' He hesitated.

'Go on,' she prompted.

'Elisa, I would do anything to prevent you further pain, and I hoped to keep this information from you. However, recent events have made that impossible.'

'Cesare, you're frightening me,' Elisa said.

He took her in his arms placing soft little kisses on her cheek.

'That's the last thing I want to do. Elisa, listen to me, remember I wanted to check out Lauren's passport and you refused to give me the information?'

Elisa nodded her head.

'Yes.'

'Well, I checked it out anyway.' Cesare looked in her eyes for a flicker of annoyance but none appeared.

She held tight to his arms for reassurance.

'What . . . what did you discover?'

'It's not good, Elisa, your uncle died three years ago.'

'Oh,' Elisa said. 'But I'm confused. What has Lauren to do with my uncle?'

'I'm sorry, Elisa. She's his daughter.'

'But that means . . . '

'Yes, she's your cousin.'

No Coincidence

Elisa tightened her grip on Cesare.

'What a horrible coincidence. I can't quite take it in.' She frowned. 'But Lauren's surname is Bradley,' she pointed out. 'I saw it on her passport. My uncle's surname is Sinclair.'

Cesare nodded.

'Her maiden name was Sinclair. She's been married and divorced.' Cesare held her close, considering his next words. 'Elisa, I'm sorry . . . there's more.'

'More? How can there be more?' Elisa raised her face to his. 'What's going on, Cesare?'

'That's what I've been trying to determine.' Cesare's jaw tightened as he spoke.

'Lauren has a brother.' He took a deep breath. 'William . . . the same William who has turned up here trying to help you sell your flat.' Cesare watched for her reaction.

'No . . . no, that can't be. You've made a mistake, Cesare.' Elisa shook her head.

'I'm sorry, Elisa, there's no mistake. I understand this is a great deal for you to take in, but the question we should ask is, why have they turned up here. It's no coincidence. What are they hoping to achieve?'

'I have no idea,' Elisa answered. Her head was spinning with the information Cesare had just given her. When she thought about it, she had never asked William's surname.

'Auntie Elisa.' Ava's excited voice sounded as Ava burst into the room followed by Fiona.

'What's going on?' Fiona asked taking in the scene and the distressed look on her friend's face.

'It's nothing.' Elisa stood up and opened her arms to Ava, who ran into them for a cuddle, unaware Elisa needed the comfort more than her.

'Doesn't look like nothing to me,' Fiona persisted, looking at Cesare for an answer.

'Elisa,' Cesare said, 'Fiona can help you but you need to let her.'

Cesare reached down to Ava, who willingly let him lift her into his arms.

'I hear your papa is coming to visit tonight, how about we go find Luigi and see if he can find some pretty flowers for you to pick and give to your papa?'

'Yes, yes.' Ava clapped her hands in delight.

'Is that OK, Fiona?' Cesare looked to Fiona for confirmation.

'Of course, thank you, Cesare. I'll make us a pot of tea, Elisa, and then you can tell me all that's happened.' Fiona busied herself keeping an eye on her friend who was looking shell-shocked as she did so.

Stella was with Luigi and they were delighted to have Ava to look after, they had grown fond of her and Ava liked nothing better than to be included with all their grandchildren as one of the family.

Cesare ordered an espresso at the bar. He wanted to give Elisa and Fiona some time together before he rejoined them. He also needed to collect his thoughts.

Someone had gone to a lot of trouble to unsettle Elisa. Her uncle had been a criminal and it looks like her cousins were, too. What about Michael — was he collateral damage or was he involved in the plotting?

Whether he was or not, one thing was clear. William was attempting to defraud Elisa, Cesare knew that for sure. His visit with Signor Ricci had been interesting and showed William deliberately gave Elisa false information in one attempt to defraud her.

Also the work done by Cesare's officers provided all the proof Cesare needed of at least another fraud case that could link to a trail of other fraudulent transactions in the south.

If Elisa met with William as agreed

tomorrow, they would probably have more proof, but Cesare didn't want to put her at risk. If she didn't attend the meeting they ran the risk of losing the very evidence that would convict him. He needed to try to find another way.

Elisa stared into her tea cup. Fiona sat beside her alternating between anger and sympathy.

'What are you going to do?' Fiona asked.

'I'm not sure, I've been trying to work it all out. Did Michael know they were my cousins? Has it all been an elaborate ploy, or has he been duped too?' Elisa said.

'Does it matter to you one way or the other?' Fiona asked.

Elisa faced her friend.

'No, not any more.'

'He's mad about you.' Fiona smiled, indicating towards the bar area.

'I'm scared, Fiona, about my new-found family and their motives, but I'm also scared that I'm falling for Cesare,' Elisa admitted.

'I know it's hard but you need to trust him, Elisa, your grandfather did.' Fiona gave her a hug.'

'Hey, look at me taking up all your time when you should be getting ready for your husband arriving.' Elisa laughed.

Cesare arrived as the friends were wiping their eyes and laughing at the same time.

'That's a good sound,' he said walking towards Elisa and wrapping his arms around her, and kissing the top of her head.

'Well, that's a sight that cheers me, and not before time,' Fiona said.

'Are you both ready to hear the rest of the story?' Cesare asked, as he and Elisa broke away from each other.

'There's more?' they answered in unison.

'I'm afraid so, but the next move is up to us.'

'I don't understand,' Elisa said.

'Well, William is desperate to have you sign those papers and now he is pushing for you to buy the land next to the hotel. He needs to move fast in case you get cold feet. His purpose is to defraud you,' Cesare explained.

'So, you have options, Elisa. We can move in and arrest him now, we have evidence from my officer in relation to another sale.'

'Another sale, what other sale? Has he done this type of thing here already?' Elisa asked.

'I'm afraid so — it's possible more than once. He made a sale the other day to a British couple. The seller was allegedly living and working in Milan. In truth, the seller was my officer Paulo, who is in fact Roberto and Jinni's brother. They like to tease him for working for me.' Cesare shrugged his shoulders. 'The house actually belongs to Roberto's father-in-law, who thinks we were using it to make a training film.

'I warned Paulo my inspector's budget doesn't run to buying a new house. So he needed to be very careful not to actually sell it to the couple.' Cesare smiled to lighten the moment.

Elisa remembered Cesare making a face at the mention of Paulo.

'Is Paulo another of my grandfather's protégés?'

'Yes, and fiercely loyal to Stephano. He is not amused at William's antics either,' Cesare answered.

'William was boasting about the sale he was keen to celebrate. How does he create the fraud?' she asked.

'Well, basically, he sets up false bank accounts and money gets transferred, whereby the client thinks all the money is in his account and by the time they realise it isn't, it's too late.' Cesare shrugged his shoulders. 'He's clever, he doesn't take all the funds, that would be noticed. It's done over a couple of days and looks like legitimate expenses but as I say the client then realises there are too many transactions, but the money has gone and only the one genuine transaction is traced back to the company as it should be.

'That's why he's desperate for you to sign papers — he knows he only has a short time before the fraud involving Paulo and the couple is discovered, so he needs to move on quickly.'

'So just arrest him,' Fiona said, 'then Elisa can get on with her life.'

Elisa watched Cesare as he took a breath and hesitated before he spoke.

'Yes, I could.'

'But?' Elisa said. 'I feel there's something you're not telling me.'

'I can deal with William, and hope he gets a custodial sentence. The problem I am concerned about is Lauren. I'm not sure of her motives and that worries me. I suspect she may be more dangerous than her brother, and to date she hasn't committed a crime. I'm not sure William has even involved her in the fraud. I think she is more of a nuisance to him.

'I watched the CCTV of her with Ava and it happened exactly as she said. A coincidence that played into her hands. However, she has gone to a lot of trouble to get under your skin, and present herself to you as a threat.

'Even the trick she pulled with Michael, and I believe she's using him, everything is gauged to unnerve you. But why? That's the question I need answered and I . . . we, may only get that answer if you proceed with tomorrow's signing.'

'Speaking of Ava, I'd better claim her back from Stella. Her daddy will be here soon.' Fiona jumped up. 'You can fill me in on what help I can give later.'

'OK, Fiona, but first I need to get out of here,' Elisa said. 'I'll make sure there's cover at reception then I'm going for a walk to clear my head.'

'I have a better idea,' Cesare said. 'Why don't we go for a drive further up the lake away from Asolto?'

'Yes, please.' Elisa smiled at him.

* * *

William shuffled papers around his desk. He would be pleased when this deal was finished. He checked his passport, satisfied all was in order, and assured himself that when Elisa's signature was on those documents he was on his way to France.

He couldn't concern himself with Lauren, she needed to deal with her own issues. Why she had come to Italy, and brought that dope Michael with her was beyond belief. Her actions threatened the whole plan.

Surely after all that had happened they were due a break in life. William screwed up his face at his childhood memories.

It wasn't until their father died that William and Lauren were surprised to discover he had inherited a substantial amount from his parents. An amount they later learned to their great disappointment he had lost due to drinking and gambling.

All their young lives, they witnessed their mother struggle to provide for the family. Their childhood had been unhappy. Desperate to find their way out of the poverty their father had caused, William and Lauren became involved in petty crime.

The other surprise their father's death uncovered was the existence of Elisa. To think their cousin had been living a life of luxury whilst they struggled from hand to mouth incensed them, especially Lauren, and she burned with determination to destroy Elisa.

William was happy to arrange for the fraudulent sale of the flat in England and now this bonus of the land deal was enough for him, he could start a new life with the proceeds of those sales.

Lauren, however, dreamed big. William knew Lauren was planning to steal the hotel from under Elisa's nose, a plan she thought William was helping her achieve.

He wanted nothing to do with her scheme, and the sooner he could get away from her, the better, as far as he was concerned.

Never Give Up

Cesare pulled the car over into a bay overlooking the lake.

Elisa sighed as she watched the sun shimmer off the surface of the great stretch of water.

'The lake never fails to calm me, it's so beautiful. I could spend hours watching over the vast expanse, seeing the ferries come and go.'

'I remember as children when we threw stones into the lake to awaken the monster.' He turned to Elisa.

'What monster?' Elisa asked.

'Ha, there wasn't a monster only my brothers and sisters teasing me.' He laughed.

'I missed all that, not having siblings. Let's go for a walk along the shore.'

As they walked Elisa tentatively put her hand in his. Cesare smiled, and lifted her hand to his lips placing a gentle kiss on the back of her hand.

'Cesare, there's one thing I don't understand. William said Signor Ricci approved the paperwork. I trust him just as my grandfather did, so has he been duped too?' Elisa raised her face to his, a frown furrowing her forehead.

'Ah, I have a confession.' Cesare smiled down at her, his eyes twinkling. 'I'm afraid I was jealous when I saw you with William.' He blushed. 'It's not something I'm proud of. It made me visit Signor Ricci though to ask him what exactly he knew about William.

'It transpires he knew very little and so I began more investigations. I figured if you were going to fall for this man I needed to know he was legitimate.' Cesare put his head to one side. 'Are you disappointed in me?'

'No, far from it, I'm glad you did. So, did Signor Ricci check him out, too?' Elisa nodded her approval.

'No, actually William tripped himself up. I believe you visited Signora Ricci, and as part of that visit you mentioned the land next to the hotel.'

'Gosh, did you have me bugged?' Elisa asked.

'No, I'm not that bad,' Cesare held up his hands to show his submission, 'but Signora Ricci was concerned enough to mention it to her husband. She was worried William was pressurising you to sign papers without her husband knowing of them. She didn't realise the chain of action she had put in place.'

'That is so kind of her to be anxious. What happened when she mentioned her concerns to her husband?' Elisa was bemused.

Cesare smiled.

'Well, when she told her husband William had spoken with the owners of the land he knew instantly William was pulling a scam.'

'How did he know?' Elisa was hanging on his every word, and despite the serious of the situation her childlike earnestness made him love her more.

'Because . . . ' Cesare paused for

effect. 'Signor Ricci owns the land.'

Elisa's eyes opened wide.

'Wow!' she exclaimed.

'Yes, wow.' Cesare said. 'And he phoned me immediately, so between us we have been watching them both very carefully.'

As Elisa watched across the lake whilst taking in this latest revelation, his mind wandered back to his meeting with Signor Ricci.

'I don't want us to scare her, Cesare,' Signor Ricci had said, 'but I'm frightened to tell her too much. She's still adjusting to all that has happened in recent weeks. This news about her cousins will be another shock for her to deal with.'

'Elisa may seem fragile but she comes from strong stock,' Cesare pointed out. 'Look what she has overcome already in her short life. Stephano did not trust this uncle, who had ruined his own life.

'He wasn't about to let him ruin Elisa's and maybe he should have given her that decision to make herself but I

217

felt he was already feeling ill and knew he didn't have a lot of time left. I guess he didn't want that time spent fighting with Elisa about a no good relative. And he was right.

'When the uncle died he probably thought he had made the correct decision, not knowing the uncle's children were bad apples like him and would come looking for Elisa hoping to make some money out of her.

'It seems they have gone to quite an elaborate plan to commit fraud rather than just present themselves to her as long-lost relatives. They must have known their characters would have given them away and Elisa would not want to be involved with them,' Cesare added.

'Just as well she has her shadow looking out for her,' Signor Ricci said to Cesare who blushed under his gaze.

'Also, that you picked up on William's boasts about the land next to the hotel.'

'Ah, that's down to my lovely wife

and her need to tell me everything about her day. Thankfully on this occasion I was listening.' Signor Ricci chuckled. 'Still, this is going to be dangerous. Are your men ready to act quickly?'

'Yes, I would trust Paulo with my life. It was he who acted as buyer for the villa in the hills to allow us to gather evidence against William. He loved Stephano for helping his family, and as a result is protective towards Elisa, and of course his family work in the hotel so he has an interest in their future.'

'Thank you, Cesare,' Elisa said cuddling into him and pulling him back to the present.

'For looking out for you?' Cesare looked deep into her eyes, questioning her.

'No, for never giving up on me.' Elisa placed her lips on his.

They stood locked together for a long time until Cesare spoke.

'I love you,' he whispered.

'I love you, too,' Elisa answered, content in his arms.

On the journey back to the hotel Elisa decided she would meet with William the next day as agreed, to sign the forms, and Cesare and his officers would be on hand to arrest him before he could transfer funds.

Cesare was reluctant to allow Elisa to be in the office alone with William. He also suspected William would place obstacles in the way if Signor Ricci or himself accompanied Elisa. William's plan rested on Elisa going to the office alone, leaving her more vulnerable if she questioned the paperwork.

★   ★   ★

Elisa arrived back at the hotel pleased to see Fiona and Ava fussing around Joe who was still reeling from all that Fiona had told him about William and Lauren.

Ava was dancing around her father listing all her favourite things about

Asolto, and the Hotel Perlino. It warmed Elisa's heart to watch her, and the little knot of anxiety sitting in the pit of her stomach diminished.

'Can you stay for dinner?' Elisa asked Cesare. 'We can eat in the apartment.' She looked hopefully at him.

'Can we have a late dinner?' Cesare asked. 'I need to get back to the station and finalise a few things before tomorrow. He lifted her hand to his lips.

'Maybe we can all eat together when Ava has gone to bed. I would like to speak with Fiona and Joe.'

Elisa nodded.

Cesare gathered her into his arms and kissed her gently.

'I'll see you later, my darling.'

★ ★ ★

Lauren watched as Cesare left the hotel. She hadn't planned for the addition of the child's father in the apartment. She texted William.

'I hope you've got this sorted for tomorrow, before we fly home. I don't want to leave any unfinished business behind.'

Moment of Truth

With Ava in bed, Elisa, Cesare, Fiona and Joe discussed the next day's plans.

'I don't like the idea of you going in there on your own, Elisa,' Fiona said. 'I could come with you. Joe can look after Ava.'

Cesare noticed the look in Joe's eyes.

'Fiona,' Joe started to say, before Elisa interrupted him.

'No way, Fiona, I'm not involving you in this. I'll be nervous enough without worrying about you,' Elisa said as she started to clear up the room.

'Well, you go then, Joe,' Fiona offered.

'No,' Cesare said. 'I think it's best if Joe stays with you and Ava, Fiona. I have police officers in place to watch over Elisa.' He turned to Joe. 'Come join me in the bar for an espresso and I'll introduce you to Luigi.'

Once out of earshot of Elisa and Fiona, Cesare looked at Joe.

'I hope you have gathered the seriousness of this situation. It's not just about getting Elisa's signature, I fear Lauren wishes to inflict further damage on Elisa. I need you to keep Fiona and Ava, especially Ava, safe.

'I shall place an officer with you, but I need you all to stay in the hotel tomorrow. I'm sure you understand I don't want to frighten either Elisa or Fiona more than is necessary.'

'Phew,' Joe said. 'Now I'm terrified.'

'I'm only being careful. I don't for one minute think she would harm either of them, but she wants to scare Elisa.' Cesare smiled. 'I'm pleased that you will be with Fiona and Ava tonight.'

When the men returned to the apartment Fiona and Joe said good-night and headed to their room. Cesare noticed the tear stains on Elisa's face. He went to her at once.

'Don't worry I won't let anything happen to you or your friends.'

'Or you,' Elisa said.

'Or me.' He smiled. 'Tomorrow is a busy day.'

He took her in his arms.

'I want to hold you close, love you and protect you for ever.'

Elisa did not believe she could love him any more than she did in that moment.

★   ★   ★

The next morning, Ava was beside herself with excitement at having her daddy at the table. Elisa and Fiona barely touched their food.

Elisa having popped into reception to check on a delivery realised a number of guests she didn't recognise were undercover officers and felt her stomach turn with nerves.

Luigi was covering reception at Cesare's request. He gave Elisa a reassuring smile, and she tried to smile back to give an air or normality.

Too soon the time came for Elisa to

leave for her appointment. Fiona hugged her friend.

'Be careful, Elisa,' she whispered.

'You too, look after Ava.' Elisa could barely speak.

The agreed plan was for Elisa to walk to the office as she would have done under normal circumstances. Her mouth was dry and her heart beat fast as she left the hotel, dressed in a simple linen dress and jacket Cesare had helped choose.

She dared not lift her head to check if an officer was following her for fear of drawing attention to him. She waved to Stella and Luigi as Cesare had instructed her. To anyone watching it was just a normal day.

As she approached the corner where the office was situated Elisa spotted Signor Ricci getting out of his car.

'Good morning, Elisa, how are you this morning, are you coming to see me?'

'Good morning, Signor Ricci.' Elisa felt her voice wobble. She didn't know if Signor Ricci was in on Cesare's plan or if meeting him was coincidental.

'No, I am meeting with William.' She didn't mention paperwork in case he asked to accompany her.

'Ah, have an enjoyable day then.' As he spoke he glanced at his buttonhole where he wore a sprig of freesia. 'Here, Elisa, Signora Ricci always likes me to wear a flower in my buttonhole.' He removed the flowers. 'You have these,' he placed them in the lapel of her jacket, 'they were your grandmother's favourites — beautiful flowers for a beautiful lady.'

'Thank you, Signor Ricci,' Elisa replied, tears in her eyes and confirmation that her grandfather's old friend and her protector was indeed part of the plan. She was grateful that she knew he would be close at hand.

Taking a deep breath, she entered the office. William, who had been watching her encounter with her solicitor, greeted her with a kiss on both cheeks, relieved she had got rid of the old man and had come alone.

'Good morning, Elisa, how are you?'

'Good morning, William. I am very well.' She looked around the office. There were two other members of staff sitting at computer desks, and a client looking at the properties for sale. Elisa relaxed, thankful there were others in the office.

'Come on through to the back office,' William suggested, 'it's a bit more private.'

Elisa's heart raced as she walked the short distance to the other room. As she entered she could see there were papers out for signing, and she hoped this wouldn't take long. She didn't know if her nerve could hold out much longer.

William also hoped to get away fast, but he continued with the charade.

'Do you wish me to go over it all page by page with you, or do you trust me?' He smiled.

Elisa's stomach lurched at his words, but she played her part.

'No, of course I trust you, William.'

'Very well, let's get these signed and then we can maybe have an early lunch to celebrate.' William smiled.

'Oh, I can't, William, I need to get back to the hotel to cover reception.' Elisa repeated her rehearsed line.

William feigned disappointment.

'Maybe tomorrow, then.'

'Yes, maybe.' Elisa smiled.

William urged her to sit at the desk as he handed over the papers with the parts for her signature highlighted. Elisa's hand shook as she signed the first paper. William was speaking but she didn't hear the words.

Without warning the door opened and Lauren accompanied by Michael stepped into the room. Lauren locked the door behind them.

'Are the papers signed?' she asked.

Elisa, unsure what was happening looked to William.

'I understood I didn't need to meet with Michael to sign the papers, has there been a change of plan?' she asked, surprising herself with her own fast thinking.

'Not that I'm aware of,' William answered, looking at Lauren.

'Elisa, I'm sorry, I didn't know about any of this, what papers do you mean?' Michael began to say, before Lauren interrupted him, laughing.

'Yeah, Michael, you don't really have much of a clue about very much.' Lauren laughed in his face.

'Lauren, what are you doing here?' William asked.

'Well, William, it's like this. Our little cousin here is a rich lady, and although we maybe could acquire some of that from these sales, I'm a bit more ambitious. I want her to pay for what her grandfather put us through.' Lauren paused.

Michael spoke.

'What has Elisa's grandfather to do with you?'

'He kept Elisa from us, oh, did I forget to share that with you, Michael, dear, sweet dumb Michael? William is my brother and Elisa is our cousin. Of course, Elisa could have contacted us when she moved to England as an adult, but no, she cut us off too.'

'Lauren, you know that's not true. Yes, she is our cousin but neither she nor her grandfather are responsible for our father's failings,' William argued with his sister.

'She is, if she had contacted him maybe thing's would have been different,' Lauren replied petulantly.

Elisa remained tight lipped. She wondered if the people on the other side of the door could hear. Were they officers, would Cesare be outside listening? Her heartbeat thumped in her ears. Keep calm, she told herself. She reckoned to try to reason with Lauren would only antagonise her.

'What do you plan to do, then, Lauren?' William asked his sister. He was growing impatient with her. Elisa wanted to know that, too, but she was unprepared for Lauren's answer.

A Matter of Life
or Death

'I'm going to kill her.' Lauren produced a gun from her handbag.

'Don't be ridiculous, Lauren. I'm not interested in revenge. I'm only interested in the money,' William said.

'Well, I want both.' Lauren smirked at him. 'When I think about our father and the life we might have had.'

'Father made his own mistakes. He could have had a good life when Gran and Grandad died, but no, he decided to drink it all playing Mister Big Man in front of his friends until it was too late, the money was gone and with it our mother — she'd had enough of his drinking and gambling.

'So, no, I don't feel any pity for him. He could have pulled himself together at that point and rebuilt our lives but instead he chose to turn to crime and that's why he ended up in jail,' William said quietly.

'Isn't that what you do?' Lauren said.

'Wrong, Lauren. I'm smarter than our father. People have a choice to take a gamble with me. Sometimes they win, most times they lose, but that's the risk they take.'

'And what about Elisa? Will she win or lose?' Lauren asked.

'Oh, wouldn't it be nice if she could win but I'm afraid she's one of life's losers. Too needy, too trusting and too naive. Look how easily you stole him from under her nose.' He tossed his head toward Michael.

'Don't remind me. He is another problem we need to get rid of.'

'We? He's your problem, and I'm not getting rid of anyone.'

'Fine, as always, I'll do the dirty work while you hide behind a desk pretending to be squeaky clean.'

'Yes, but at least I don't pretend I want revenge for our father when what

I really mean is I'm eaten up with bitterness and jealousy because I didn't enjoy the lifestyle I felt I was due to me.'

Lauren shot him a look and he knew he had hit a nerve.

'Why shouldn't I want more in life? It was a stroke of luck to find details of poor little rich girl's mother, our aunt, in amongst father's meagre belongings along with that letter from her grandfather giving him a pay-off to keep out of her life.'

Elisa felt her stomach turn. Nonno had used his hard-earned money to keep her uncle away.

'If only the grandfather had died before our father it would have been far easier to pull on her heart strings instead of this elaborate scam,' Lauren continued.

'Ever the sympathetic heart, Lauren. What an inconvenience to you the poor old man enjoyed a long life. Maybe if she hadn't caught you with Michael and you got your hands on his flat like we had agreed by scamming him, then things would have been easier, and we could have taken our time acquiring the hotel,' William argued.

Elisa felt a trickle of sweat run down her back as William and Michael both made a move for the gun. Lauren was too quick for them, and pointed it at all three of them. Elisa prayed Cesare would not try to burst into the room.

'Don't try that again, anyone,' Lauren said. 'The plan is we will all make our way to the ferry pier. William, you will lead with Elisa, keeping a close eye on her, in case her interfering boyfriend shows up. Michael, you will walk behind with me, and don't try any heroics or she gets it.

'When we're on the ferry and moving across the lake, Elisa will have a dreadful and unexpected fall overboard. The ferry will do the rest and the lake will finish her off. Then you and I, William, will lay claim to her estate, being her only surviving relatives. How shocked they will all be at our grief for our long lost cousin. To have accidentally found her and then lost her to a tragic accident so soon.'

'What about me?' Michael asked.

'What about you?' Lauren seemed to suddenly remember he was in the room. 'You come with us, but any funny business and you'll follow her overboard. Right everyone, let's go.' Lauren indicated with the gun towards the door.

They did as Lauren instructed. Elisa's legs shook as she tried to move them. She was aware they wouldn't inherit from her due to the change in her will, and was thankful for Signor Ricci's foresight.

She didn't think Lauren would be receptive to this information in her present state.

Elisa prayed they would be spotted going outside, but hoped the officers would keep their distance. She didn't want anyone to put their lives in danger because of her.

Whatever happened, she knew Lauren would not be successful in stealing from her again. She was not the same girl who arrived in Italy, upset and broken-hearted.

She was stronger now, surrounded by people who loved and supported her, and capable of standing on her own two feet and running a successful business.

Lauren threw a shawl over her arm, covering the gun, and followed them out of the door, past the staff who continued with their work, seemingly unconcerned.

The short walk to the ferry pier seemed to go on for ever. The normality of the lake with ducks and swans grabbing at pieces of bread thrown at them seemed to pass by in slow motion.

The everyday sounds of the busy cafés and bars echoed in her ears as though they were coming from far away.

Keep calm, she told herself, keep walking.

Eventually they were on the pier

amongst the others in the queue, most of whom were excited holidaymakers. Lauren had purchased the tickets in advance, leaving no opportunity to move away from her. Elisa was scared to move in case Lauren in her emotional state fired the gun indiscriminately.

The sun beat down on them and Elisa could feel perspiration trickle down her back. Her eyes searched the crowd on the pier seeking out Cesare. He promised she would be safe — where was he?

Once she boarded the ferry Elisa feared she wouldn't come back. As she walked forward she gazed into the water surrounding the ferry and calculated if she could safely jump in before Lauren could react, this could be her only way out, and prevent anyone else from being harmed.

The queue started to move as the passengers boarded, the blue uniformed crew members shouting instructions, urging passengers which direction to take. William and Michael moved on to the gangplank. Elisa, following, took a step forward.

Without warning there was a rush of movement around her and she heard shouting. Cesare dressed in crew uniform appeared from nowhere and grappled Lauren to the ground.

Elisa turned around to discover the line of passengers behind her had been held back by officers and those she thought were fellow passengers in front of her had grasped William and Michael.

She turned back to Cesare who was handcuffing Lauren, and handing her over to two officers to drive back to the station.

Elisa felt her legs go from under her and she reached out, Cesare caught her in his strong arms.

'I don't understand. How did you know what her plans were?' she asked.

'Well, we didn't really know what she would do. We had two officers stationed in William's office, and when they saw

Lauren we knew she had to get you out of there if she had any chance of staging an accident. We reasoned she would head to the airport or the ferry. The mike you were wearing bought us some time to get to the ferry and set up for you arriving,' Cesare answered. 'We had to move very fast.'

'I'm grateful you did, thank you. Wait a minute, what mike? I'm not wearing a mike,' Elisa said, confused.

'I suspected you would be uncomfortable wearing a mike, and we didn't want to risk you being self-conscious and possibly give the game away as a result.' Cesare lowered his head, nervous of her reaction. 'So, we sneaked one on you.'

'We?' Elisa asked.

'Well, Signor Ricci, actually.'

'Signor Ricci, but how? Oh, the flowers!' Elisa touched the small bunch of freesia and felt a tiny metal button attached to the ribbon wrapped around them.

'Yes, the flowers. We could listen in

without you being aware and uncomfortable about what you were saying, and thank heavens we did.'

'Can they hear us now?' Elisa asked.

'Yes,' Cesare answered and made to move towards the flowers.

Elisa side stepped him and smiled.

'Good, because I love you, Cesare Favero, and I don't care who hears it.' Elisa lifted her head and Cesare gratefully obliged her with a long lingering kiss as everyone on the pier applauded.

Happy In His Arms

Later that night Elisa studied Cesare's face as he dozed peacefully in the armchair after their eventful day. Ava and her parents had gone to visit with Stella and her family at Stella's insistence to let Ava play with her grandchildren, and to give Elisa and Cesare time alone.

'Why are you watching me?' Cesare asked, smiling, with his eyes still closed.

'Don't flatter yourself. I'm not.'

'Yes, you are.'

'OK, I am, but it's not because I love you or anything.'

'Yes, you do.'

'I don't.'

'You do, and you always have.' Cesare opened his eyes and reached out for her.

As she moved into his arms she knew he was right. She loved him as much as she loved this hotel and town. She was home and the depth of love she felt was like a key turning in a lock — everything just fitted together. Her grandfather's words came back to her — everything will click into place.

The only problem she still had to face was the hotel's future, and she still needed to meet with the staff, and that frightened her as much as William and Lauren.

Elisa remained worried about the timing of her meeting after the incidents of the previous day that had resulted in William and Lauren's arrest, and Michael being put on a flight home, but she reckoned the staff could cope with one more shock.

She looked around the room at the assembled staff and into the faces of people she had known for years, and knew what she was about to say would change their lives for ever.

The previous evening, she had spoken at length with Signor Ricci and Cesare. This morning she spoke with

Fiona and Joe to fill them in on developments.

She smiled at Cesare standing by the door offering her encouragement just by his presence. Signor Ricci sat at the table with her ready to help answer any questions that might arise.

'Good morning, everyone.' She started to speak and her voice wavered slightly at the sight of the anxious faces before her.

'Good morning, Elisa,' Stella answered back loud and clear and everyone followed on with their greetings giving Elisa the courage to continue.

'I would first of all like to thank you for all your hard work and dedication given to my grandfather and the hotel.'

There were a few murmurs from the back of the room, people trying to anticipate what was to follow. They quietened as Cesare glared at them.

'I realise this has been a difficult time for you and your families given the uncertainty of the future of the hotel, so

I really appreciate that standards have not dropped, and you have all gone the extra mile to serve our guests as always, and in particular when Ava disappeared. Thank you for your quick reactions.' She cleared her throat.

'I am sorry you have been forced to wait for me to come to a decision about the future of the hotel.' She paused. 'As you know, Hotel Perlino was built by my grandfather, Stephano, and you also know of the great loss he and my grandmother Rosa suffered, their family wiped out. No son left to continue the name or carry on the business.'

The room was hushed.

'I came across a letter from Stephano the other day,' Elisa continued, 'and it reminded me of the great community that this hotel and the village was and still is. When they were at their lowest the community pulled them through, and I know there are many people who also benefited from Stephano pulling them through, too, when they needed help.'

There were nods from one to another as people remembered Stephano's kindness.

'So I have a favour to ask,' Elisa went on. 'I ask if you, the community that is Hotel Perlino, will pull me through, as I take forward plans to keep Hotel Perlino open and carry out the expansion plans my father and grandfather dreamed of for the hotel to be open all season and cater for skiers, mountain bikers and summer holiday makers.

'It will be a lot of work for all of us — including my friend Fiona and her family. In recognition of this, Signor Ricci has helped me draw up contracts that will, depending on length of service, allow you to become part owners of the new extension as a thank you for the loyalty you have shown to our family.'

The room erupted, and Elisa was showered with kisses and cuddles.

'Oh, my little potato.' Stella hugged her. 'This is wonderful news! Stephano would have been so proud of you. Luigi, our dream has come true.' Stella turned to hug her husband who had tears in his eyes.

There was a rush around Signor Ricci as people wanted to find out more.

'That went well,' Fiona said.

'I think it did, and now the real work begins if we are to open for next season,' Elisa said. 'I am so happy you and Joe have decided to join me here. There's a lot of work to be done, and between you, Stella and Jinni you will be in charge of getting everything set up. Joe and Luigi will project manage.'

'Well, Joe is very good at what he does, so he'll be in his element, and thank you for offering a job to my dad, too. They are delighted to be able to be near Ava.'

'Well, you are all my family, and when they see how happy Ava is here, they'll know you made the right decision.' Elisa hugged her friend.

'Hey, can I get one of those hugs?'

Cesare appeared at her side.

'Of course, fiancé.' Elisa turned to kiss him. 'Oh, no!' Elisa clapped a hand over her mouth. 'I forgot to share our news. I was so nervous about the extension plan.'

'Everyone, can I have your attention again for a moment please? I forgot to tell you. Cesare and I are engaged. So we also have a wedding to plan.' Elisa laughed.

There was a roar of approval.

'It's about time,' Stella added. Everyone joined in laughing and congratulating the happy couple.

Cesare wrapped her in his arms.

'I was never going to let you slip away for a second time. No matter where you chose to live.'

'That will never happen again, my love. I'm going no further than your arms.' Elisa reached to receive his kiss, and to begin their journey of a lifetime of love.